About the Author

J. S. Andersen was born into a family of artists in New Mexico, USA, whose creativity rubbed off on them since a young age. Being diagnosed with attention deficit disorder, their mind never stopped racing or creating worlds. After many long years, the decision was made to channel that energy into creating the world of Sura for their debut book, *Free Are the Wicked*, in the hopes of highlighting the importance and dangers of societal ostracism, and that everyone deserves a chance, regardless of who they are.

Free Are the Wicked

J. S. Andersen

Free Are the Wicked

Olympia Publishers
London

www.olympiapublishers.com
OLYMPIA PAPERBACK EDITION

A CIP catalogue record for this title is
available from the British Library.

ISBN: 978-1-83543-127-6

First Published in 2024

Olympia Publishers
Tallis House
2 Tallis Street
London
EC4Y 0AB

Printed in Great Britain

Dedication

I dedicate this book to Devin Ayers, the first teacher to see promise in myself.

Acknowledgments

Thank you to my wife Katy for encouraging and supporting me throughout the writing process.

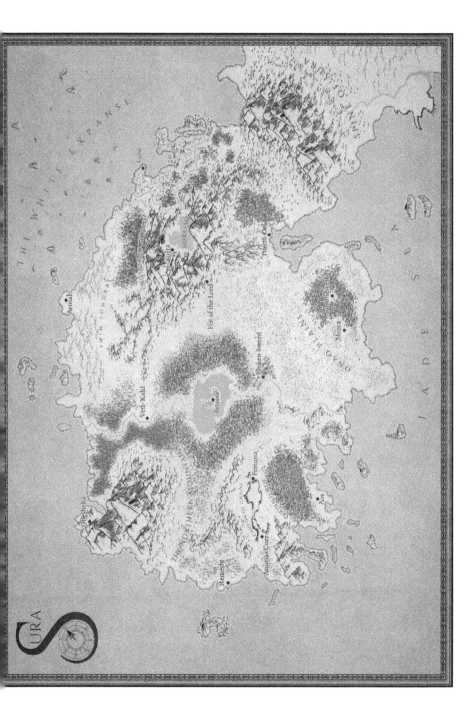

Chapter 1

The world doesn't need a hero, it needs a sacrifice. Only to appease the unknown like a dark forest. Those few chosen were never given a chance, as I soon wouldn't be. But I was the forest, and it was winter.

I shielded my eyes as I looked up toward the sky. The relentless sun was beating down on me as I walked aimlessly down the dirt road. This was the only road, really, in this small hamlet I lived in. I had nowhere to go, nothing to really do; I was unemployed, as were most of the people here. I had friends that I had grown up with, but they had all left for varying reasons. Most of them, however, went to join The Church of Sura.

"I'm going to help stop the Sages," they all said, in hopes of creating a better life for their families, for their towns, probably even the whole region. Sages are those 'unlucky' enough to be born with special powers and said powers can be anything; from causing tsunamis or even just making the soil more fertile for crops. Everyone seemed to fear them. They were the blame for all of society's downfalls, such as famine, crime, even poverty. The Church has made sure to make them the boogeyman, labeling them as 'Abominations to God.' It's ironic, really, because in the past, being a Sage meant social status. Families would even have arranged marriages in order to procreate an even stronger Sage. That was a long time ago though, in a vastly different world than what I have known.

They were exceedingly rare now, and if I'm honest, I'm

surprised there are any left at all. Most people go out of their way to try and report any suspected Sages to The Church, as they have offered hefty rewards for any information for a Sage's whereabouts. Of course, everyone jumps at the opportunity, it is the only real opportunity that any of them could make decent money in their lifetime. I'm sure The Church had good intentions, but, as I'm sure one could imagine, it just turned into a witch hunt. So many people were being accused, whether they were an actual Sage or not. But The Church would pay every time. Even just last week, a girl in my hamlet was accused. The Church promptly sent a mission of their own out and made quite the show of her public execution. She kept crying and saying she was innocent, that she has never had any powers. No one even knew what the supposed powers she had were; not that anyone cared. The Church had brought one of their own Sages with them, one of the 'Chosen' who had been turned to a holy purpose. It was the first time I had ever seen a Sage in person; I was in awe, their silver-gilded robes draped to touch the dirty ground, a large hood draped over their head. I remember they stood there, silent, looming, menacing. Everyone gawked at them, including me. Once the Church official had read their religious passage, they brought forth that local girl, chained up, gagged, and bruised already from being beaten in captivity. I never knew her, only saw her at her father's food stall next to the blacksmith I worked at, where I'd spend hours polishing and doing menial tasks. I wasn't sure what to expect; I'm not sure anyone was, because we all witnessed the Sage raise their hand toward her, a scarred, mutilated-looking hand, and in a flash, a shot of lightning came cracking out of their outstretched fingers. I couldn't look away; I couldn't believe what I was seeing—to see someone have the kind of power that crashes out of a terrible storm. I just remember her screaming as they electrocuted her repeatedly, until... she was silent. I felt sick; I had just watched someone die in front of me. Her skin was smoking, burned, cracking. I will never forget that smell. Several in the crowd yelled "Justice!" but I couldn't shake the feeling of if they were wrong, if she was telling the truth.

That was only last week, but it already seemed like ages ago. The man who accused her, Rodrigue, was given his sack of money afterward, then quickly disappeared. And here I was, walking down the same road that it had happened on, with no evidence that she had ever existed. That whole incident should have made me feel safer, at peace, but it made me terrified. My whole childhood I kept having moments where I would question if I had powers as well, if I was a Sage. I would always see people, talk to people, but no one else could see or hear them. Sometimes at night, they would come to me; sometimes, they'd try to talk, but most of the time they would just stare. It scared me as a child, and whenever I would try to ask my parents about it, they'd just tell me I have a vivid imagination.

I had to keep pulling my torn, stained shirt over my shoulder to keep it out of the sun; I wish I could afford new clothes. My feet had grown tired from walking and my home was on the edge of town, so going to and from was a chore. Nothing made me realize how much of a dead-end life I was living quite like this commute. I stopped underneath the shade of an overhanging building. An old, rotting wooden bench had beckoned to me off to the side, the same building covered most of it in the shade— good enough for me. There was an elderly man sitting on one side of the bench already; he was dressed very nicely, professionally, with an umbrella keeping his balding head out of the sun. I didn't want to be near anyone, but I didn't care at this point. I sat down next to him, trying to stay as far on the opposite end of the bench as possible. I tried not to look over, instead looking up at the building bordering the road I had been walking on. So many had started to decay, their wood frames rotting, or holes in the walls and missing windows. This used to be a bustling mining town, but ever since the mining disaster, the town has been in financial ruin. There was no real economy anymore, and most of the mine's workers were locals. Those that could afford to get out did. The ones that couldn't...

I glanced over at the man next to me; his clothes were in immaculate condition, not a speck of dirt on him. How is that possible? I looked up at him, studying his posture. He sat perfectly still, with just a blank stare straight ahead. Was he waiting for something? Someone? Why was he here of all places? To my horror, he glanced over at me, noticing my inquisitive gaze. He turned his head toward me, but I quickly looked away, pretending to study something in the distance. He let out a low, exhausted chuckle. I sat there, mortified, calling myself an idiot repeatedly in my head.

"So, where are you headed?" I froze at his question. I regretted sitting down here; I hated being near strangers. My own family wasn't nice to me, why would someone I didn't know show me any kindness?

"*Uh...* N-nowhere, actually." *God, why did I have to stutter!*

"*Ah...* Well, I suppose that makes two of us." I looked up at him, confused.

"The way you're dressed, it sure seems like you have some important business. Like you have plans to go somewhere," I blurted out without thinking, instantly regretting what I said in fear of it coming off as rude.

"And where, pray tell, should I be going?" Another

confusing response.

"I… don't know."

Neither of us said anything more, just staring straight ahead, me being as confused as ever. The sun was continuing to beat down on me, the true reason I despised summer.

"What's your name?" he asked, breaking the silence.

"Sid. What's yours?"

"*Ah*, Sid. You seem to be quite the gifted person."

I furrowed my eyebrows, confused and unable to tell if he was being genuine or mocking me. This man was so strange; nothing he was saying was making any sense. I noticed a couple of patrons stopped walking in front of us, staring at me; they also looked confused. Brushing it off, I turned back to the elderly man next to me.

"You didn't tell me your name."

"Well… that doesn't matter now."

"What do you mean that doesn't matter?" I was invested in finding out more about him; if it delayed me returning home, then I relished the opportunity. No one had ever bothered to hold a conversation with me, except…

"You'll understand one day. I just enjoy simply… being." I didn't respond, I had nothing else to say. The two patrons, a man and a woman, started looking even more confusedly at me. Why were they looking at me specifically? Was it my clothes? Probably. They looked rather tattered, and I'm sure my hair was a mess too.

"Do you always just sit here?" I finally asked him.

"No."

"Do you live nearby?"

"No."

God, this was becoming frustrating.

"Okay… then is there anywhere you want to go?"

Why did I care so much? It was probably because this was the only genuine conversation I've had with someone recently that didn't involve anger or hatred.

"I would give anything to see my daughter, actually."

"Then why don't you?" Suddenly, one of the confused strangers shook my shoulder, making me jump. I whirled around to see the man that been watching me from the street. He looked rather disheveled too, his hair thinning, and his breath stank. I pulled my shoulder away, showing I was visibly annoyed, and he stood back. I've always never been able to hide my emotions.

"Are you all right…? Who are you talking to?" Confused, I held up a hand, pointing to the man next to me.

"What do you mean? I'm talking to hi—" I froze; when I looked over, that man was gone.

"There's… no one there. I've been watching you talk to yourself. Are you all right?" I nodded and jumped up, quickly walking away, embarrassed.

It had happened again; I saw and talked to someone that no one else could see. *It's been happening more and more frequently. Why was it happening though? Is this really my imagination? It can't be… they're all so real.* The dirt crunched underneath my feet as my mind was running rampant, trying to understand what just happened. The most frustrating part of it all was that I had no one to confide into, no one to talk with safely about this. I was so scared that these might be signs that I have a power but… what kind? We've all heard stories of the different kinds of powers that have existed throughout history, but I've never heard of anything like this. Was something wrong with me…?

Eventually, the dirt road turned into an unkempt path, full of weeds and larger rocks. This signaled my turn-off was coming, much to my dismay. Once I reached the path that led to my home, I stopped and took a deep breath. The sounds of the town I passed through were but whispers now, and the hot breeze blew through my hair. I knew I had to come back; I didn't have anywhere else to go. My legs grew heavy as I forced them to move once more. Slowly coming upon my home, I took note of the same things I did every time: the cracking foundation, the rotting planks in the walls. Home was supposed to be everyone's sanctuary, their haven. But for me, it was my hell.

Chapter 2

The neglected exterior of my house loomed before me. It wasn't the smallest or most decrepit in our town, but the lack of upkeep had certainly been showing, almost as a peering glass into the state of our lives. I could've turned around, I could've just left, never come back. My family probably wouldn't notice, not at first, anyway... but where would I go? I had nowhere else, no one else. I think they might know that, too, that I'm virtually trapped with them, much to their dismay.

I took a deep, shaky breath; the weeds were probably growing around my feet by now from how much I had been hesitating. I took the heavy first step and walked through my front door. Like clockwork, my father was sitting at the kitchen table. I remember it being a beautiful piece of furniture when I was younger, the ornate and stained wood looked like an art piece, proudly displayed in the center. Years of heavy use and neglect took its toll on it; the wood was cracking, the stain was peeling off, as well as the paint that had been applied on top of it. It became a regular sight, my father and that table, with him slumped over it, several empty bottles accompanying him. We made eye contact, but no words were spoken; they never were. He went back to staring at the peeling wood, probably doing his best to drown out the verbal abuse my mother was throwing at him. *Ah* yes, my mother... The constant emotional and verbal abuse she attacked him with was also a mainstay in our home. He would always just ignore her, and I never knew how he could have so much patience; but now that I'm finally an adult, I realize now it's not patience, it's depression. It had been this way my entire life, her anger bellowing out, lashing at him. They resented each other, and all it created a toxic environment that I had to grow up in.

My father worked at the quarry just outside town, where most of the population here worked. We were never poor; we've always had enough money to buy what we needed growing up and put food on the table. My father, however, was not the best at managing his finances, and it showed. He'd blow it on bad investments, gambling, or personal hobbies. It had made us destitute. That was what my mother attacked him over the most, her expectations of us being wealthy with his high position at his job. I couldn't stand it; I just wanted her to be happy with what we had. I know she could be a great mother, a great role model, but her mood could change at the snap of a finger. I just wanted her to be happy. Maybe then our lives would be…

No, there was no point in spiraling down that rabbit hole. It was never going to change, and I knew that. Call me a hopeless optimist, I guess.

I had to get away, and quickly retreated into the hallway toward the bedrooms. I don't think my mother even noticed I was there. I sharply turned around the corner, wanting to scurry away to my room like I always did. But as I quickly came around, I bumped into something that made me stumble back. I quickly looked up, to see my sister, Allison. Her annoyed glare shot daggers through me, and I instantly felt the heat from embarrassment cover my face.

"Watch where you're going, Sid."

"Sorry." I couldn't muster anything else to say before she pushed past me, heading out to where my parents were, her shoulder-length dark brown hair flowing behind her in her stride. We used to be close, my sister and I. Growing up, she was my best friend, and I wanted to be like her. She was so stubborn and hard-willed, which is probably viewed as a negative trait to many, but I admired her for it. As we got older though, we started drifting apart. We became very different people, looking at others and the world from two different looking glasses. She was a stranger now; I could barely recognize her; even the fact that I was taller than her was foreign to me. No more 'looking up' to her, literally and figuratively. I never knew what to say anymore to try and rebuild the relationship. She never made an attempt anyway, and I felt anger toward her for it.

I took one last look behind me at the rest of my family, the chaos making me cringe. I wanted so badly to tell them what happened to me today at that bench—what I had been haunted by my whole life. But I knew I couldn't; I knew what could happen if I did… become a villain, a criminal, a 'Pagan.'

Was I really one of them? A Sage? Or 'Pagan' as the Church labeled them now? No, there's no way. They were almost extinct now, and I've heard stories of what they could do in the past, like controlling the weather, the oceans, or even disease. I had never heard of anyone like me. And besides, what could I even do? Hear and see the dead? I had brought it up to my mother when I was very little, when I first started having these instances. She just mocked me, told me I was imagining things or that I was being dramatic. Before it was few and far between, a sporadic voice or an object falling here and there. But then when I was either fourteen or fifteen, I had a horrible nightmare of being pulled down underneath the ground by hundreds of corpses and gasping for air as the dirt slowly covered my face. I awoke, drenched in sweat and gasping. I looked down at my hands that were throbbing in pain, and they were covered in dirt, my fingernails scraped away, as if I had been clawing at the dirt, just like in my dream. The most alarming part of it all though was when I finally saw my reflection; my eyes were blue my entire life, but now they were a bright violet hue. As I got older, the experiences had become more frequent, more alarming, more... terrifying.

I would see shapes at first, shadows. But they became more and more defined as time went on. Now I saw people, just as real as everyone else around me, just like the old man on the bench earlier today...

I didn't know what was happening, I was scared, and these instances were making me feel even more alone, more isolated. What scared me the most, though, was that I had never had a conversation with... one of them before. They would just stare at me or yell something incoherent; but lately, they have been yelling my name. It was never the same person either, always someone different. Sometimes, they'd look like a normal person, but other times, they would be disfigured, mutilated, and I had been assuming that must have been how they died.

The past two weeks were especially bad. Nearly every night, there would be dozens of them clawing at my bedroom window, constantly yelling my name, yelling to let them in. I haven't been able to sleep and it was affecting my well-being. They wouldn't let up, no matter how hard I yelled at them to stop. My room had become my only sanctuary growing up, the one place I could get away from everything and isolate myself. But now, because of them, I was losing that part of me as well. The sky outside my window caught my eye, the beautiful streaks of orange and pink signaled that an anxiety-inducing night was coming. I dreaded going to bed now, to the point I had started trying to keep myself awake for as long as possible, hoping to delay the inevitable.

"Hey."

I jumped; I must have been zoning out for who knows how long.

"Oh, hey." Allison was leaning into my doorway, looking confusedly at me.

"We have to go to the square early tomorrow with Mother for the sermon, don't you remember?" Oh right, that God-damn sermon. Every month, the Church would have a priest come by and deliver their 'sermons' to every town, preaching about God's will and their mission to protect us from the unholy and unclean. It was just a vain attempt to stroke their own ego, and I saw right through what it really was; a show just to display that they're the ones in charge.

"Yeah, I remember," I groaned, looking down at the floor.

"Then why are you still up?"

"I'll go to bed in a minute, I swear."

After a disapproving look, she disappeared back behind the door frame, and I heard her door slam shut. Shit… I really did have to just face my fear now. I don't know what would be worse, not sleeping through that torment or my mother's rage in the morning if I hadn't slept. I stood up and stared at my window, trying to psych myself up just to be able to climb into bed.

"Okay… stop being a coward." I climbed into bed reluctantly and pulled the sheets over my head. The warm embrace of my blankets felt so welcoming, I hadn't realized how sleep-deprived I had become over the past two weeks. Before I knew it, I had drifted away into the night.

*

I jolted awake to loud banging and screeching sounds, like nails against glass. I threw my sheets off and jumped out of bed, still trying to wake up and get my bearings. Once I had snapped out of it, I realized what was happening, and my stomach dropped. I slowly turned around; they were back. My window was rattling from how hard they were pounding against it. There were even more this time, so many covering my window I couldn't see even one crack of darkness from the outside. The constant pounding and yelling wouldn't cease.

"SID!"

"OPEN!"

"SID!"

I clamped my hands over my ears, attempting to block out their screaming. But I could still hear them in my head. How could I hear them so clearly in my head? That's how they never woke anyone up; they weren't yelling out loud, they were yelling at me. I couldn't stand it anymore, so I clenched my teeth and crouched on the floor.

"SID!"

"HELP!"

"LISTEN!"

I couldn't get away, I couldn't run. My stomach started turning, and I felt sick from the fear welling up inside me.

"NO!"

"WHY?"

I panicked and whirled around, facing them with tears running down my cheeks, infuriated.

"SHUT UP!"

I threw an open palm at them, and an icy jolt shot through my body and through my outstretched arm. A violet cloudy vortex erupted from my hand, growing and smashing through my window, taking all the dead with it. Their screams started growing distant and faint as the dark swirling clouds sucked every one of them in, before it finally collapsed in on itself and disappeared altogether, leaving a thunderous crack and rumble.

I stood there, shocked, staring at the now-perfect circle in my wall where my window once was. I couldn't move, I couldn't believe what I had just witnessed. I stared at my hand; did I just do that? How did I...?

"What the hell was that?"

My mother came running into my room, glaring at me. Fear overwhelmed me as I saw her rage when she realized half my wall was missing. She stood there, her mouth hanging open, in silence.

"What... what did you do?"

"I... I don't..."

"I said what did you do?"

She came charging at me, grabbing the candlestick holder from my end table and swinging it at me. I threw my arms up to protect myself, but it didn't work. The metal bottom struck the side of my head, sending me falling to the ground. Pain shot through me, and my ears started ringing.

"How the hell are we supposed to fix that? How are we supposed to pay for that?" she yelled as she repeatedly kicked me while I was on my floor. I didn't even try to say anything to defend myself, just tried to stay in the fetal position to protect myself the best I could.

She finally stormed off, leaving me coughing on the ground, my head throbbing. I started crying; I wanted it all to end. My emotions ran through me like a horse. I was so sad, upset, defeated. But then finally, angry. I had grown so angry. Angry that I had to deal with this, angry that I was crying, angry over how hurt I had let myself become. But most of all, I was so angry at how I hadn't tried to do anything about my situation. I knew now, I did have some kind of power, and it was taunting me, taking control of me, and my fear was letting it win. I showed myself what I could do now; I could win, I could become more. I opened my eyes, my vision so blurry from the tears I couldn't make anything out. I slammed my fist onto the floor, making my decision. I wouldn't let the dead or my family torment me. *I will escape this, no matter what it takes.*

Chapter 3

I awoke to the sound of birds chirping and the freezing morning air filling my room. Opening my eyes made me realize how much pain I was in; I had slept on the hard floor. My blurry vision finally stabilized, and I saw my biggest regret—the giant hole now in the middle of my wall. I glared at it, still trying to come to terms with what I had done. I could hear the birds singing happily outside. I lay there still, staring longingly out into the world. It was almost tormenting mc, tcasing me, like some cruel joke the world was playing on me, knowing I had been longing to be free of this hell I had found myself in—free like those birds, able to live their own lives.

I rolled over onto my back, the pain shooting through the shoulder I had been awkwardly laying on. I knew I had to escape, to get away. But… how? I stared blankly at the cobwebs on my ceiling, hoping maybe some inspiration or idea would spring into my mind. If only I had family elsewhere, or friends… or if the Church wasn't ruling with an iron fist, I could escape. Maybe I could just leave… Would they even notice? Or care? Maybe not. I suppose I could very easily walk out that door and never come back. So why haven't I? The obvious answer was, I was too scared. Too much of a coward to be that bold and take my life into my own hands. Being told your whole life how much of a failure you are doesn't exactly inspire confidence…

I let out a loud groan as I sat up, the pain spreading from my shoulder down my back and up my neck. I glanced down at my shirt, my tears and snot had stained it now, mocking me with how pathetic I was for crying so hard. I had to change my clothes. I let out an audible groan as I forced myself up from the floor, my legs wobbly for a second as they adjusted. I pulled my shirt off angrily and threw it onto the floor in frustration. I never wanted to look at it again. I stood there and wanted to yell at the top of my lungs, clenching my teeth and shutting my eyes. I hated feeling so helpless. I tried to calm myself down with a heavy sigh. I guess it worked, at least a little bit. That was all I really could do here, lest I cause another scene unintentionally. That's when the thought shot into my mind, I had made a scene. How did no one else hear? We had neighbors. Did everyone turn a blind eye? Or was it not as loud as I remember? No, it was loud, booming. Someone had to have heard.

A chilling breeze snapped me out of my trance, and I realized I had been standing in front of the hole in my wall without a shirt on for the whole world to see. I quickly jumped back toward my dresser and swung it open, I had to find something to wear, I didn't know how late it was already, and I couldn't risk angering my parents any more than I already had by missing the sermon. I riffled through the clothes, finally deciding on a dark blue tunic I had stuffed in the corner. I was always fond of this one; the blue matched my eye color. I threw it over my arms and slid it nicely down to cover the rest of my body. The sleeves were lined with a silver fabric, nicely complementing its dark color. The only thing left was to tie my brown belt around the waist, completing my look. I never had any sense of fashion, but I couldn't complain about this outfit. Looking down at my pants, they didn't seem too dirty, which was surprising since dirt always showed up on black fabric.

Okay, I said to myself, trying to psych myself up for the

challenge of having to deal with the inevitable showdown with the rest of my family. I threw my old boots on and slowly meandered out of my doorway. I could hear low mumbling coming from the kitchen; it was my parents no doubt. I couldn't make out what they were saying or if they had an angry tone of voice. I paused before turning the corner, my heart already racing and the anxiety already building. I closed my eyes, quietly saying to myself how screwed I am. Before I could convince myself otherwise, I turned the corner into the kitchen.

The muttering stopped, my parents and my sister were all there, staring at me. I could cut the tension with a knife.

"I didn't miss the sermon, did I?" I muttered, desperate to break the silence.

"No... we were about to leave without you," said Allison, striding toward me. My mother jumped up from her chair, sending it sliding back with so much force that it almost toppled over. It caught Allison's and my attention, making her spin around.

"You better tell me the truth about what you did last night," she barked.

"I... I don't know."

"How can you not know? I had two neighbors at the door last night asking what all the commotion was. You made me look like a fool because that's all I could tell them also." So, others HAD heard. I broke eye contact and looked at the ground, shaking my head angrily.

"We're already late, we need to leave," Allison spoke up, seemingly already annoyed. My mother broke her glare away from me and stomped through the doorway to the outside, my silent father in tow. Me and my sister followed next. I never wanted to go to these; I seemed to be one of the outcasts who didn't express their love toward religion. Not going to sermons, however, would only cast you in a bad light, which could be deadly nowadays.

My mind ran rampant and consumed my thoughts as we walked to the town square. I didn't remember any of the trek over. But once we found ourselves in the crowd, I looked up at the rotting, wooden stage to see one of the priests. His tan robes with red, gilded trimmings flowed down to just above his feet, his elderly skin was clean and properly cared for, unlike most of us in the audience. Two soldiers from the Church stood by his side, watching us. Their armor and weapons shining brightly in the morning sun. Their appearance of 'clean and holy' were just selling points to view them favorably. Afterall, who would want to be dirty and poor when you could have nice clothing and be clean like them?

"Blessed be the light that illuminates not only our skies, but our lives," the priest started, raising his arms outwards toward us. My mother pushed me and my sister forward, forcing us to get closer to the stage until we were only several feet away.

"We come not only with joyous intentions, but hope. Hope that we will one day be born to a most delightful land, free of the damned, conspirators, pagans. For these abominations hide amongst us still. But fear not, the holy Church of Sura fights tirelessly to bring peace and prosperity to each and every one of you." The crowd nodded in agreement, with the occasional "blessed be" being yelled out.

"No more do we suffer from war, sickness, hunger. Because our Lord has made it so. But our work is not yet finished, not until the last pagan has answered for their crimes of defying our God with their... abilities." A couple of people spat on the ground at the mention of Sages. I shook my head. Everyone

31

seemed so bought in to the thought of a loving 'Lord' and Church. How could they think that knowing that others had to suffer for it? For just being born?

"The discovery of a young girl being a pagan in this town has brought great sadness to all of you, including myself. I mourn with you all. But the Lord has filled my heart with the hope that we bring with us. Blessed be!" he exclaimed, nearly everyone in the audience also yelling those affirming words back.

"They pray to a light that will bring them no warmth," I muttered to myself, visible anger appearing on my face. My mother jabbed me in the back for saying that, and I noticed the older woman next to me was looking at me as well with a shocked expression on her face. Only just then did I realize who she was, our neighbor. A very devout woman who would often invite us over for prayer. I looked away, crossing my arms and scoffing.

A hand grabbed me and pulled me back, my mother whispering, "How stupid are you?"—to me as she shoved me forward, signaling it was time to leave. I walked in silence in front of my family, and we soon reached our house.

"Are you trying to make us look bad in front of everyone?" she yelled as she slammed the door shut behind all of us. I turned to look at her, not saying a word.

"Well? Are you just going to stand there looking like an idiot and ignore me? What is wrong with you lately?"

"I told you I do not know!" I reacted, shouting at her. My anger had reached its tipping point and was getting the better of me. I could feel myself shaking. I couldn't tell if it was from anger or fear.

"Do NOT talk back to me like that!" she shouted back, now angrily striding toward me clenching her fists. I jumped back; I knew what she was planning on doing, exactly what she did last night. I wanted to run, I wanted to hide, crawl and wither away in fear like I had always done… My anxiety was causing me to tremble even more, I couldn't move. She got a couple of pounding steps closer to me, and I felt my arms start to feel a familiar cold run through them.

"DON'T TOUCH ME!" I yelled at the top of my lungs, reacting by throwing my open hands downward to the floor. Everything moved in slow motion, and the floor rumbled. Before I could take another breath, a dozen blinding white lights burst from the floor, breaking the floorboards and sending them flying throughout the room. They took shape and manifested into… people. They were surrounding me, but not facing me. I gasped and looked around at them, then came to the realization; they were facing my mother. Were they… protecting me?

"What… what is this?" shouted my mother, nearly falling over from how hard she was back pedaling. My father shot up from his chair, his mouth agape in disbelief. My arms still felt cold, like this power was flowing through them. I didn't know what to do, I stood there, also in shock with what was happening. I knew I had to leave; I knew I had to run. I glanced over at Allison, who had been knocked to the floor. We made eye contact, and she gave an almost approving glance, like she was… relieved. I took one look at our front door and bolted toward it. I ran through the spirits I had summoned, their white aura nearly blinding me as I passed through. I threw the lock open and burst my way outside and ran to the end of my street. I keeled over, not realizing I hadn't been breathing and started to desperately suck in air. I glanced around, realizing I had been standing in the middle of the main street.

"There! That's him! He's a Sage! He destroyed his home and mocked our prayer!" I spun around, seeing our elderly neighbor pointing her withered and aged hand toward me from down the road. To my horror, I saw who she was talking to – soldiers from the Church. They had made their way down from the stage already, and she obviously jumped at the chance to rat me out to them. God dammit, why did I have such bad timing to let my powers get the better of me? Four of them immediately started charging toward me, drawing their swords, indicating there were going to be no questions asked. I turned and started running as fast as I could with no direction or thought about where I had planned to escape to. I could hear their armor rustling as they shouted at me to stop, calling me a heathen, pagan, and every other swear word they could think of. I knew running on the road would be a death sentence, I was sure to run into someone else associated with the Church. I had to think, I had to plan, but the sheer panic was making me not be able to think straight.

I finally saw my exit – the forest. Of course! They didn't know its lay about like I did; I had the advantage of playing there my whole childhood. I stopped to look behind me, seeing them still giving me chase. Without hesitation, I jumped off the dirt road and bolted into the dense trees.

Chapter 4

The sound of crunching leaves bounced off the trees that were flying past me; I was in a full sprint, trying to jump and dodge every which way like a cat, desperate to lose my pursuers. My heavy panting soon overwhelmed the other sounds of the forest, and I was almost positive they could hear the panic in my breaths as well. I darted behind every decently large bush or tree, but to my frustration their footsteps would always catch back up to me. I had to create more distance, but I didn't know how I was supposed to do that. Could I use my powers? Should I stand and fight? No, I have no control over them, I don't know what would happen, if anything at all. I couldn't risk it, not here.

My plan to evade them in the golden trees I grew up with was failing spectacularly, and I was starting to find myself in unknown territory as I ran further and further in. The trees were growing taller, their trunks becoming more and more massive. I had known that this sprawling forest kept these giants as a well-protected gem, but to see them in person was breathtaking. It almost made me want to stop and stare up in awe; they had to be hundreds of feet high, only allowing the sun to shimmer through, which just added to their beauty.

I had to snap myself out of it; I was being chased, I had to find some way to escape. My throat burned as I was gasping for air and my legs started becoming weak. I don't know how long I had been running for; it felt like hours. The realization was setting in, I was going to be killed. It's bad enough to even be born as a Sage, but to run? That was practically a death sentence. I'm sure they would just chalk it up as fighting back. I had to decide soon; I was rapidly approaching my limit on how long I could flee, and I was learning that I wouldn't be able to escape them, no matter how long I dragged this out. Maybe I could bargain with them, plead, or beg. Maybe there would be one of them with an ounce of humanity left in them. There had to have been a near zero chance of any of that working; I couldn't imagine the punishment they'd face if they willingly let a Sage go.

I had to stop, I had to do something. I tried to stop myself and almost tumbled, my legs nearly giving way. I didn't realize how exhausted I was until I stopped; my whole body felt like it was on fire, and I couldn't suck in the air fast enough. I keeled over, putting my hands on my knees, trying to peek behind me to see how close they were. Sure enough, they were sprinting up toward me in the distance. With a loud groan I forced myself upright and turned around, ready to muster whatever power I could use. I had no idea what I was doing, but they didn't have to know that.

Finally, they reached me and stopped, drawing their swords and pointing them at me from a couple of feet away. They were barely even winded; it was almost insulting.

"I'm only going to say this once," one of them started.

"Surrender yourself to the Church, or you will force our hand. You must know you have nowhere else to go."

I clenched my teeth. It wasn't much of an option; be killed now or surrender and be killed later. I outstretched my arms downward and opened my hands, trying to mimic the same thing I did at my house in front of my family. I focused as hard as I could with my head pounding. Sweat dribbled into my left eye, causing me to shut it from the stinging. I kept trying to feel some inclination of power through me, but there was… nothing.

The soldiers stepped closer to me, clearly agitated at my silence.

"So be it…" one of them slowly started to raise their sword, clearly intending to strike me down. Before he could swing, a blinding streak of light flew past my head and struck the soldier in the forehead, followed by several more. They all hit the same mark; every one of the soldiers was struck in the forehead by these arrows of light, sending them tumbling to the ground. I stared in shock; I couldn't believe what I had witnessed. The arrows dissipated, leaving only small holes with a narrow streak of blood pouring out. They were dead. All of them, instantly snuffed out before me. I noticed a couple of my hairs laid on my arm; the first arrow must have sliced right through them and missed me. Did it miss? Or was I intentionally spared? I stood there frozen, staring at their corpses as their eyes were still wide from fear. A footstep crunching on leaves echoed close behind and jolted me back to reality. I whirled around ready to defend myself, but to my surprise, there stood two young women. They were both tall, nearly as tall as me. The one on the left's hair was so blonde it was nearly white, that she had pulled back into a messy bun. She was so pale, and her green eyes were also piercing from how light they were. The other one to her left was almost a direct contrast, who had a darker, mocha complexion. Her hair cascaded down like a black waterfall, covering her shoulders and down her back. Her face was captivating, striking. They were both studying me, not breaking their gaze from mine.

"So, why were they chasing you?" the girl with the white hair asked.

"I… I don't know." I didn't want to be honest with them, I

didn't know who they were or if they were a threat to me. She looked annoyed and crossed her arms.

"You don't know why Church soldiers were chasing you?" I stayed silent, still feeling nervous about these new strangers. They didn't seem threatened by me at all.

"Well, good thing we helped, or you would have led them right to us," the black-haired one finally said, breaking her silence. Good thing they helped? So, they were the ones who shot out those arrows of light? One of them was a Sage then! Or maybe both.

"Right, well, good luck with that then." The white-haired one reached down and picked up her pack off the ground and threw it over her shoulder. Several large, golden leaves behind kicked up and gracefully fell back down to the ground. She beckoned for her companion to follow.

"Wait!" I nearly yelled without thinking. They both turned around, looking back at me surprised.

"They were chasing me because... I'm a Sage. I think." They were my only chance, and if one of them was as well, maybe I could find common ground. They turned around to face me, as if suddenly interested in what I just said.

"Can... can I come with you? I have nowhere else to go, I can't return home." I almost begged, I was so desperate. The white-haired girl just scoffed.

"No. We already have enough to deal with. We don't need a third Sage with us." I knew it, they were both Sages, and they looked like they were on the run too.

"And no offense, but you clearly can't defend yourself, I'm not going to babysit you." Wow, those words stung. But she was right, I couldn't defend myself. I had no idea how to control my powers. I had felt powerless all my life as a matter of fact.

38

"We can't just let him get killed out here, we have to look out for one of our own. He has his best chance sticking with us," piped up the black-haired girl.

"I said no, we can't risk it," she snapped back, turning and starting to walk away.

"And what if I had let you hang?" She raised her voice at the white-haired girl, causing her to stop in her tracks. After a tense minute, she finally looked up at the tree line and let out a loud, heavy sigh.

"Are you from around here?" she asked, turning her head slightly.

"I… yes. I grew up in this area."

"Do you know this place? It's like a damn maze."

"The Golden Forest? Well… yeah, for the most part."

"Fine. Just… try to keep up," she finally said, turning around and looking me dead in the eye.

"I'm Mars, by the way. And this is Otto." I looked over, the black-haired girl was lifting the flap covering the top of her pack she had slung over her back and saw a Gray and white cat sticking its head out, staring at me.

"I'm Sid." I gratefully grabbed her hand, shaking it. I felt a massive weight lift off my shoulder. Maybe I'd actually have a chance sticking with them.

"And I'm Bastien," said the white-haired girl. I gave an affirmative nod.

"So, where are you two headed?"

"Fortuna. You've heard the rumors of Sages being smuggled out to escape through there, I assume?"

"Well… yes, but those are just rumors, aren't they?"

"We have reason to believe there's more to it than being an old wives' tale," said Bastien, adjusting the strap of her pack on her shoulder. I looked at the ground. Fortuna? That place was just a cesspool of crime from what I had heard. Mars strode past me toward the bodies that still lay strewn across the forest floor. I watched her bend down and pick up one of the soldier's swords, inspect it as it glistened in the sunlight, and sheath it through her belt.

"I for one am eager to get moving," said Mars, quickly striding past me. Bastien gave her and myself a nod, and I followed behind them, unsure of what the future might bring for the three of us.

Chapter 5

The leaves crunched softly under our footsteps, and I kept catching myself looking up in awe at the size of the flora around us. It didn't seem real, and I couldn't help but ask myself why no one would venture this far from my town? Maybe they were scared, or just didn't have any reason to, unlike me. The loud chirping soon broke the eerie stillness of our surroundings, almost as if a hundred birds had become aware of our presence. Periodically, you'd see one fly in between branches, or swoop low past you. I've always loved bird watching; my mother and I would go do that in our spare time at the edge of the forest. Of course, once I got older, that time of bonding stopped.

A brightly colored Blue Jay swooped in between two of the mammoth sized trees, its feathers only exuberated by the trickles of sunlight sneaking through the thick canopy. I had only been able to take in my surroundings for about an hour now, and I had already seen more than one type of bird I had never seen before. As I followed in silence behind Mars and Bastien, I noticed more than once that Otto was also just as invested in bird watching as I was. Every time a bird would whisk by, he'd nearly jump out of the pack and let out a huff and plop back down. I almost enjoyed watching him as much as my surroundings.

A black and white crow-sized bird had swooped down barely missing me. It made me jump; I hadn't even seen it coming. Otto jumped out and had his front paws on Mars' shoulder, ready to show that bird what he was made of, but alas, it was long gone.

The cat's sudden lunge made Mars turn her head and look at him, the first time her and Bastien's conversation had been broken.

"How are you doing?" she asked.

"Oh, I'm fine." She reached back and scratched behind the cat's ear.

"I mean, I was asking Otto, but that's good you're doing well too." I felt my cheeks flush, I just showed them how awkward I was.

"So, how long had you been on the run before you ran into us?" she added on, probably noticing how I wanted to die from embarrassment.

"Only a couple of hours. I'm from a town just outside this forest." I beckoned in a vague direction behind me, but I had absolutely no idea which way Aos was.

"Does that mean you know this area beyond here, then? Past the trees?" Bastien chimed in, stepping toward me.

"I only know we're in the Golden Forest, but none of us ever ventured fully through; so no, not really." I saw the disappointment shown on both of their faces, making me realize that they didn't have a map, or a path set out; they were just winging it, much like I was when trying to escape the soldiers. Mars patted Otto once more and opened the pack for him, gently stuffing him in there. She turned to face Bastien, presumably to decide how much longer they should walk for the day. But before I could contribute, a vine wrapped around a nearby tree broke off and reached out to Mars. I whipped my head toward it, amazed at what I was seeing. The vine reached her pack and… clasped it shut for her before falling to the ground.

"What the hell?" I exclaimed, still looking at the motionless vine. Mars looked over at me confused, and followed my gaze to the ground, seeing the vine and letting out a chuckle.

"Oh, that's right, we never talked about this did we?" I looked up at her, surprised at her laughing, trying to decide if it was my bewilderment, she found amusing.

"Plant-life, that's my thing. I can control them all, and we speak to each other," Mars clarified.

"You... made that vine close your pack?"

"No, I just asked it nicely, and it obliged." She smiled at me, visibly holding back laughter at my mouth gaping open.

"Bastien though, she's the one that saved you, so you probably owe her a 'thank you.'" She beckoned over, who had crossed her arms, showing her impatience.

"I... Right. Thank you," I stammered, still trying to collect myself.

"Don't mention it."

"So, you can throw those... arrows?" I asked her, curious as to what her powers were.

"Sure. But really, I control light. I can shape it and make it take on whatever property I desire." She held out an open palm and created a small swirling ball of light, before snuffing it out under her closed fist.

"And you?" Mars asked, breaking my trance from Bastien's hand. I looked down at my own hands, still trying to comprehend what it even was I could do, but I guess I owed it to them to try my best at explaining.

"The... dead. I can see them, communicate with them. And until recently, I summoned them, as if they were under my command. But it was by accident, and I still don't know how I did it. That's actually what got me exposed, and why I had been on the run." I looked back up at them, and they looked at me, shocked. My gaze darted between the two, wondering what the big deal was.

"I've never... heard of anything like that," Bastien said, quietly. I looked at her, and shrugged, not sure what to say.

"To be fair, I've never heard of your powers either, Mars," I finally said, breaking the shocked silence.

"And yours, Bastien... wasn't light one of the past Viscount's powers?" I added on, hoping for clarification. She only met my gaze, and slowly nodded. Did I say something wrong? She didn't seem too thrilled to have the same power as the head of the Church from a century past.

"Actually, I've never heard of either of you. I'm guessing you two aren't from here?" The burning questions had finally started flowing out of me.

"No, we're not. My family moved around a lot, wherever my father found work. Most recently I'm from Puerto Del Sol," responded Mars, who then shot a look over to Bastien, waiting for her to answer.

"... Artessa," she begrudgingly said before looking away. She's from the capital? And has that power? There had to be more to her than she was letting on. I looked back at Mars, who met my gaze.

"I was in Broken Sword and saw her in the town's square, she was up on the gallows and was about to be hung." Bastien looked over, suddenly interested in how Mars would tell the story.

"The Church, of course, exclaimed she was a pagan, and 'an abomination to god,'" she added on, using her fingers as quotation marks.

"I don't even know why I felt compelled to but... I saved her. I made a tree erupt from underneath and destroy the gallows. So, we've been on the run ever since, much like you."

"Yeah, and you sent me flying. I'm lucky I didn't break

anything," Bastien chimed in. I looked over at her, then to the ground. I thought my experience was harrowing, I can't even imagine. Mars telling me that story made me realize how far behind I was in controlling my powers as compared to them. But maybe they've known about them for years, whereas I've only just truly found out about mine. We fell in silence before all of us realized the sun was starting to set. After discussing, we decided it was best to try and set up some sort of camp for the night. After rounding up enough twigs and bits of wood, I stacked them up the best I could. Bastien reached past me and put her hand on the pile, igniting it with a bright glow. The warmth soon flooded the surrounding area, and I hadn't realized how cold I had been until that moment.

"I've actually never heard of a girl being named Bastien, if I'm honest," piped up Mars, who was sitting crossed legged on the ground with Otto sleeping on her lap. I guess they were also learning about each other, they must not have been on the run for very long either.

"That's because I was supposed to be a boy. My father was convinced I was going to be. And when I was born a girl, he just left the room. Probably to a tavern or something to drown his misery."

"Oh… I'm sorry, I shouldn't have been so ignorant."

"No, its fine, I don't mind. In fact, I never saw him until I was about seven or eight years old, when my powers started showing up. Then he finally took an interest in me, wanted me to be some 'prodigy' in the Church. I'm sure it was only to further his political career though, fathering a child with the same power as a viscount? He loved it."

"So then… what happened?" I butted in.

"A lot. I got sent to become one of the Church's 'chosen' but lashed out and badly injured a cleric. Got myself a one-way ticket to Broken Sword for it."

"Why didn't your father help?" I added on, trying to piece it together.

"Don't worry about it. We need to get to sleep, it's getting late." I couldn't argue with her there, it was only getting colder, and I was completely exhausted.

The other two unrolled blankets they had strapped to their packs and quickly covered themselves before finding a somewhat comfortable position to lie down. I sat there with my arms crossed, trying to keep myself warm with what little amount of wood was still burning in the fire. I was woefully unprepared and didn't have anything with me. I closed my eyes and told myself how much I wished I had at least brought a thicker shirt.

Something jolted my eyes open as it smacked me in the chest. I looked down, seeing another tattered blanket still rolled up. My gaze shot up, seeing Mars sitting up, her arm still outstretched from tossing it at me.

"Take mine, I've got another. Goodnight, Sid."

Chapter 6

I felt cold, as if a strong wind had been blowing through me. I tossed and turned, desperately trying to find warmth. I reached out my hand to pull my blanket over my head, but there was nothing there; my hand grasped at air. I opened my eyes, confused, and was shocked at what I had seen. There was… nothing. I was lying in a black void. I quickly sat up, gasping. My gasp echoed throughout the darkness. Where was I? What is this? I was interrupted by the sound of splashing water as I moved my legs. I was lying in a shallow bed of water, but it was also black. I lifted my hand out of the murky liquid; I didn't appear to be wet at all, and my clothes seemed dry. But whatever this liquid was, it was so cold that it sent a familiar chill through my body. It felt the same as when I had channeled my power back home, before I ran away… I jumped up to my feet, wanting to get out of whatever this was that was covering the ground as far as I could see. Spinning around, I noticed that I was completely alone here. I could feel an energy emanating from me, almost like I had so much power at my fingertips. This chilled tingling feeling in my hands, was this my power that I had felt before? It felt so much easier now, like I had control over it so easily.

Looking up from my hand, I decided trying to use my power here wasn't going to do any good; I needed to find a way out, wherever out was…

"Hello?" I called out. My ragged breaths were all I could hear as I anxiously awaited a reply. Honestly, maybe it was a relief I didn't get a response. I looked around for another minute or so, trying to decide where I should try to look for an escape. I only took one step before I heard it, a low rumble. I froze in place, trying to figure out where it had come from. My head and body were spinning around, desperately trying to see through the thick darkness, my feet splashing in the shallow water.

I heard the rumble again, only this time it was louder, and almost sounded like a growl, echoing from the darkness. I couldn't pinpoint where it was because it seemed to come from all around me. I had to do something, I had to defend myself from whatever it was. But before I could react, the ground gave way, I fell through the water, and it overtook me. I was falling, the liquid rushing past me. My yelling made me realize I could still breathe as I free fell.

I jolted up, gasping. My vision was blurry from the sunlight trickling in from the canopy above. I rubbed my eyes, still trying to catch my breath. Looking around, I saw Mars and Bastien looking at me, surprised. They had already had their belongings packed up and were sitting on the fallen log from the night before.

"Bad dream?" asked Bastien, taking a bite from some bread she must have been carrying. What was that just now? Was it really a bad dream? It must have been but… It felt so real.

"… Yeah, sorry." I rubbed the back of my neck, feeling embarrassed for causing a scene. Mars reached into her pack and pulled out some bread wrapped in linens.

"Here, we saved this for you." She reached out, handing me the loaf. Seeing the food made me realize how hungry I was. I couldn't remember the last time I had anything substantial to eat. I swiped the bread from her hand and began devouring it like some sort of feral creature. Even though it was just a plain loaf, it was delicious, and my dreadful mood instantly lifted.

"Thank you, that was actually really good." I wiped the crumbs from my shirt, trying to make myself look halfway decent again.

"Well, you're easy to please," replied Bastien, who just now finished hers before neatly folding the linen it was in then stuffing it inside the pocket on the side of her gray tunic. She stood up, making eye contact with Mars as if for confirmation.

"So... we were talking while you were asleep. This power of yours... You claimed you could control the dead?"

"I mean... yeah. I don't fully understand it, but yes."

"So how does that work?"

"What do you mean?"

"I mean, can you hear the dead? And see them? Like, are they always there?" she asked, vaguely gesturing around us. It was a good question, and the answer was both yes and no. I sat there for a moment, trying to figure out how to explain it all. I stood up, adjusting my rumpled tunic, their gazes following me.

"Only when I'm needed. I know they're always there, like hands clawing against a glass window. I don't see them. Unless I look." I looked around, past the other two as I said it. It was true, I knew the dead were around us, I could feel them nearby.

"I guess talking always just sounds like noise until you actually listen," replied Mars, who was now standing up as well. Even Otto looked like he had been brought to attention as he was now sitting up on the log next to where she had been sitting.

"You said you can control them, right? And you don't really know how to do that?" asked Bastien. I looked at the ground, but all I could give her was a nod. I felt embarrassed admitting that. They seemed like they had so much control over themselves, and here I was, fumbling through life.

"How did you feel when you did control them? What

emotions?" she added on. The question made me shoot my gaze up at her, confused.

"*Uh…* anger. And fear…" I tried to recall the feeling I had when I was back home, the anxiety that had built up inside me just from my mother raising her voice. I didn't seem like that should be the reaction I had, but I guess I have been conditioned to respond that way my whole life.

"So, pretty strong emotions then. Maybe that's it. I'm the same way, I can open the flood gates to my powers when I'm feeling anything strong like that."

"And I'm the opposite. I need a clear and calm mind, otherwise the plants seem to ignore me," Mars added on, smiling at me. Maybe Bastien was right, my powers really erupted whenever I was feeling some sort of distress.

"Fight me then, let's see if you can conjure up anything," Bastien interrupted me, stepping toward me. I stepped back, shocked. Fight her? There's no way, I had watched her kill those soldiers, she'd wipe the floor with me. I stopped and collected myself, maybe this was the best way to figure this all out, especially now that I had an idea of how to control myself.

I gave an affirmative, "Okay." And we took a couple of steps back from each other. I closed my eyes and tried to envision my home life, my parents yelling at me, trying to capture that dreaded feeling I always tried to escape from. A subtle "vwoom" sound made me open my eyes, only to see an orb or light strike me in the abdomen, sending me flying back and colliding with a tree trunk. I gripped my left arm in pain, it took the brunt of the force. Bastien stood away from me, still holding out her index finger toward me, another ball of light manifesting at the tip of it.

"Let's go, Sid, we don't have all day." She challenged me. I noticed that this orb was bigger than the last, and was vibrating intensely as it grew in size, casting shadows everywhere around it. It was almost blinding; I could tell this one was going to be excruciating. I clenched my fist, suddenly scared of the pain I was about to feel. Bastien cocked her arm back, ready to fling it toward me.

"No!" I yelled, out-stretching my right arm toward her. A bitter chill ran up my arm and throughout my body. And then I saw it, a ghostly hand manifesting out of thin air behind her arm, grabbing it and yanking it back before dissipating. She stumbled back, her orb shimmering away as it was interrupted, and looked back in shock. I lunged forward, opening my hand in a desperate attempt to prevent her from charging that up again. A swirling funnel of violet clouds came erupting from my hand, engulfing her and sending her flying back. It all seemed to happen in slow motion as I watched them cover her body. I started to let out my breath I had been holding, but a blinding whip came ripping through the tunnel and wrapped around my neck. I grabbed at it with both hands, dissipating anything I managed to conjure up. The whip pulled me closer, my feet dragging against the ground as I flailed helplessly against it. I opened one of my eyes to see Bastien laying on the ground, propped up by one of her elbows, holding the whip in the other hand.

"Well, that sure was something, wasn't it?" she said, amused as the whip disappeared from around my neck. I fell to the ground, clutching at the burning feeling it had left. Footsteps came up next to me and I looked up, seeing Bastien holding out a hand to me.

"I think we found what drives your power after all." I brushed the leaves and dirt off myself as she helped me up. That felt... great. Like I was one step closer to being in control of my life somehow.

"We really need to get going; we've wasted enough time." She beckoned, walking back over to Mars. While packing everything up we all chatted about how we all felt our powers could keep growing and eventually continued our path to Fortuna.

As we kicked dirt over the fire from the previous night, I heard a snicker and spun around. I didn't see anything, only the swaying trees in the wind. I was about to ask the others if they heard that, but before I could speak, another snicker, this time from my left. As I jerked my head to look, I saw it. A tiny, yellow creature was peering at me from around the trunk of the tree, about twenty feet high. It looked like a tiny person, with pitch-black eyes and small wings on its back. But then another appeared from behind the adjacent tree, except this one was pink. They were… smiling at me.

"Oh. Pixies. They've been here for a couple of hours," Mars said, walking up next to me. She must have heard them as well.

"Pixies…? Why are they staring at us?"

"Probably just want whatever we leave behind. They're little scavengers. We should probably leave quickly though; I don't think they're very patient."

"Leave quickly? They're tiny, what could they do?" I asked, looking at her confused.

"Well, they're venomous. Real nasty stuff. So yeah, we should probably go." And with that, we grabbed the rest of our belongings and set off.

We had been in the forest for a while now. I would have guessed we should be out of it, but maybe we were close to the end, we had to be. I wanted to take in the sights of these trees one last time, the sounds and stillness of the forest. It still seemed so bizarre to me that a place could exist that was this peaceful and serene with all the turmoil going on in the world. Well, I guess it was only turmoil for anyone who was unlucky enough to be born a Sage. It was strange though. I didn't feel unlucky to be born one; I felt blessed. I suppose that's just what the Church has conditioned you to think, that Sages were "abominations in the eyes of God." A line I had heard way too many times over the course of my life.

Chapter 7

My legs and feet ached from walking so much in the past day or two. I tried to just keep my head down and zone out, falling in a mindless tandem behind the other two. Maybe it would make the trek shorter by disassociating. But every time I thought I was falling into an absent-minded walk, something would jolt me back to reality, whether it be the flapping wings of a bird flying away, or a stick snapping. I shouldn't have been so hyper-aware of every little noise but fearing for your life makes you nervous about everything, as if at any second everything could go wrong. It was mentally draining. I felt like an empty shell.

"What exactly is the plan when we get there?" Mars asked, breaking the numbing silence around us.

"I don't know, we're just going to have to improvise and figure it out when we get there," replied Bastien. It wasn't much of a plan. But as stated before, it was better than nothing. I was hoping, almost praying we would reach the end of this forest. The overgrown path we had found seemed to lead us in the direction we wanted. It clearly hadn't been used in quite a while; in fact, I probably would have never found it if Mars hadn't. The serene stillness I was in awe with earlier was turning into a personal hell. The silence made this forest stretch on endlessly. I envied Otto, being able to be carried around in a pack while you were dozing off, letting life take you wherever it pleased. That freedom of burden sounded so nice.

"I don't think I've really seen a lot of cats around, where did you find Otto?" I asked, finally thinking of something to say to them. Mars turned her head and gave me a quick glance before facing forward again.

"My father is a general laborer. Or builder, I guess you would say. He travels all over to construct buildings. That's why we moved so much when I was growing up, wherever his work took us." Her pack started rustling around, Otto must have woken up. It was as if that cat always had a reaction to her voice. I couldn't exactly blame him, it was soothing.

"And one day, about two years ago, he comes home with this little runt of a kitten. He found it underneath some rubble at his work site. Apparently, he was the only one still alive." She looked back and smiled at me.

"I begged him to keep the kitten, and I named him Otto. We've been inseparable ever since." It was a weird thought to have, but I was thankful she was willing to be so open with me. Maybe she trusted me enough already, or maybe I had just been so conditioned to believe that every question I had was met with negativity in my life.

It was touching to hear that her father and she had saved him. I was surprised they had even found one; I think I may have only seen one other cat my whole life. When the fever started breaking out, a lot of superstitions and hearsay were being thrown around, which spread like wildfire. None I don't think caught as much traction as the rumor that cats carried the fever and spread it. There was no proof of that, and I'm not sure where it started, but that didn't stop people from hunting down the poor animals. An ill-timed exchange of words can be just as deadly as any blade.

After what seemed like an eternity, we all saw it. The sunlight was starting to break through the canopy more and more. The trees were clearing! I looked ahead, anxiously waiting to see where we would end up. I was ready for a change of scenery, ready for the sun to finally hit my skin and warm me back up. It was ironic; I hated the direct sunlight back home, but now I couldn't wait for it to be back. Suddenly, the three of us stopped. It wasn't a meadow or some pristine mountains; we were standing at the top of a cliff. The wind whirled around us as it shot up the cliff face, the sunlight making us all squint. I cautiously stepped past the other two, shielding my eyes. Off in the distance, I could see what looked like... a settlement? Or town? The wind was whipping up so much dust in the desert below that it was difficult to make out.

"Is that... Fortuna?" I asked, pointing out what I was seeing.

"It has to be." Bastien stepped up next to me, also squinting at the town in the distance. I knew Fortuna wasn't exactly a welcoming place, but that town looked neglected. I suppose every location in the western part of this land looked neglected. It was blatantly obvious the capital Artessa never looked our way, as if the western half was the forgotten stepchild. We had always heard of how beautiful and extravagant the eastern cities and towns were. I accepted long ago that I would never witness such places. If this desert slum was going to be where we found salvation however, then I guess beggars can't be choosers.

"Okay, so... how do we get down there?" I asked, addressing the obvious problem we now face. We all looked around, but to be honest I'm not sure any of us knew what we were looking for.

"Hey! Look!" Mars shouted, pointing to a stone cairn on the edge of the cliff in the distance. It was as good of a lead as any as we all quickly made our way over to it. She was right to call it out, as we saw a decaying and ancient looking wooden ladder. It was only about ten feet tall and led to a narrow path that seemed to traverse along the cliffside heading to the desert below.

"This has to be a joke," Bastien said, annoyed as she knelt inspecting the ladder. It was held up by two corroding iron spikes which had dried out leather straps wrapped around both poles of the rotting wood. She pulled one of the straps and it cracked and broke immediately. Sighing, she stood up, clearly trying to come to terms with the path we obviously had to take.

"We need to get moving. Just don't look down," Mars said, stepping past Bastien and slowly putting her foot on the first rung. The ladder groaned as she cautiously took one more step down. At first glance, I would think she wasn't scared, but I could see her hand trembling as she tightly gripped the sides of the ladder. After an anxiety ridden minute, she finally reached the bottom and looked up to us, beckoning at us to hurry.

"Okay… let's just get this over with." Bastien took one more deep breath and cautiously began her descent as well. The ladder groaned even louder now. She reached the bottom and put her hands on her knees, meaning it was now my turn. After a couple of choice expletives ran through my head, I gripped the ladder as hard as I could and started to ease my weight onto the first rung. I don't know why I did, but I looked behind me, seeing at how perilous this really was. If that last strap gave way, there would be nothing holding me or the ladder in place. It would just be a free fall for several hundred feet. I tried to calm myself. I hated heights. But I knew I had to just hurry and get off this thing. The next couple of rungs were uneventful, but a loud burst of wind shot up from underneath us and startled me. I twitched, which made the rung under my right foot crack and nearly give way.

"Hurry!" I heard one of them yell through the howling wind. I almost lost my grip, but the panic made me move even faster. I hurriedly jumped down, the hard landing hurting my feet as I stumbled away from that accursed thing.

"I thought we were about to lose you," said Bastien as she grabbed my arm to help me regain my balance. I didn't reply, I was just thankful I made it.

"It looks like this trail is a switchback, just be careful, this wind isn't letting up." She was right; it was howling louder than ever. It did not make walking on this narrow path any easier. I pressed on behind them, anxious to get the hell off this cliff. I hated every second of this part of our journey, but I was glad they were there with me. It was calming to know that they were looking out for me. I hoped they knew I was looking out for them as well. The steep incline made my knees howl in pain and I had to constantly try to adjust my footing so as not to slip on the dirt trail that was carved into the cliff face. Whoever made this, they did a poor job of it. We all stayed silent and focused after what seemed like an hour or two of traversing this descent. We all slipped a couple of times, but thankfully caught ourselves before we could fall and tumble. I know I envied Otto before, but not anymore. I couldn't stand having my entire life in the hands of someone trying to keep their balance on the side of a cliff. Finally, to the relief of everyone, the trail leveled out, and we were reaching the end. The scorching heat was starting to set in as we were finally able to focus on something other than our impending deaths.

Soon, the hard-packed dirt gave way to loose sand. We made it. I had never been so happy to see a desolate hot wasteland like the one we were in. We all ran off the end of the trail, all letting out a relieving sigh. The second we did, the wind suddenly died down.

"Oh, of course, the wind stops now. It's like we're being pranked," said Bastien, holding her arms out to show how annoyed she was.

"Well, yeah, we're Sages. God hates us remember?" replied Mars, making herself and Bastien laugh. I hurriedly ran in front of them, ready to lead the way for once and pull my own weight.

"Come on, I can see Fortuna, it doesn't look that far." I beckoned. The mounds of sand made it difficult to move quickly, but I didn't care. I don't think anyone cared; we were so anxious to reach our destination. As we trudged forward, several families of quail scurried in and out of the desert bushes around us, with the occasional rabbit or sand fox watching us carefully. Their orange and brown fur made a nearly perfect camouflage. In fact, I wouldn't have seen the foxes if not for the occasional flicking of their two tails.

It was like a dream come true. We were so close to finally being able to get help, to be able to escape this place. My legs burned, but I pressed on, the other two in tow behind me. I could see the town getting larger as we neared, until eventually the stone arch loomed over us, signaling the entrance inside. I stopped, looking up at the faded and chipped bend above us. My previous observation on the cliff couldn't have been more wrong; this place was full of life. Even from the outside, I could see people walking about, and merchant stands in the middle of bustling crowds, laughing and talking.

"Well, are you two ready?" I asked, turning around. They were also observing the crowds as I was. They both nodded at me, and we walked side by side through the archway.

Chapter 8

The flurry of earthen-colored tunics quickly engulfed us as we slowly made our way into the plaza. Dust and dirt were being kicked up every which way by the residents, some in cloth shoes and others barefoot. It was easy to get overwhelmed by the shouting and talking, many of which had a heavy dialect that was hard to understand. This was clearly the central hub for all things mercantile, with the haggling and adverts being shouted over the crowds. The amount of activity in this seemingly forgotten town was shocking.

A hand firmly gripped my shoulder and shook it, making me whirl around, only to see Bastien beckoning me to follow her. I tried to press my way past everyone surrounding me, being bumped into by people hurriedly striding past. How could someone live with this chaos? I had been here for five minutes and was already wanting to leave. I struggled to keep her in my sights, and she led me and Mars around the corner of a building, thankfully away from the crowds.

"I can actually hear myself think now." Sighed Bastien, adjusting her hood to try and keep as much of her face hidden as possible. Half of our clothing was already stained from the dirt and dust, which I suppose would help us blend in more.

"All this noise would actually serve as good cover for something like a Sage smuggling operation, if you think about it," Mars replied, taking another look back at the plaza. Bastien simply nodded as she attempted to pat herself down, sending small clouds of dust off her, but it didn't make much of a difference.

"We need to ask around, try to see if someone knows something."

"Yeah, obviously, Sid." I gave an annoyed look at Bastien as she snapped at me. She stood back up, giving up on trying to smack the dirt off her and saw my reaction.

"Sorry... I just don't like crowds. This is stressing me out." She sighed. I understood where she was coming from. Growing up in a tiny quiet village was the opposite of this, and I realized it was stressing me out as well.

"Why don't me and Sid see what we can find? I know you'll probably say you work faster alone." Mars stood next to me, and Bastien nodded in agreement. Thank the lord, I didn't want to have to deal with this on my own, I wouldn't even know where to start.

"All right, let's meet back here in an hour then." Bastien gave us both quick glances to affirm we agreed, then she quickly darted down a nearby alleyway. Me and Mars both turned to once more face the plaza, taking deep breaths seemingly in unison.

"Well... first things first, I'm hungry. Let's see what they have to eat around here, yeah?"

"Yeah but... I don't have any money." I agreed with her, my stomach was growling as well. I looked at her puzzled, only for her to smile at me.

"Don't worry, I've got that covered." She patted that glimmering sword she had taken from the dead soldier in the forest. I reluctantly nodded, completely unsure of what she meant by that or what she was planning on doing. With those last words, we set off into the crowds.

Both of us had our heads on a swivel, trying to see just what kinds of stands and shops were around us. Many of the signs I didn't recognize, as several of them had different symbols and writings in a language I did not recognize. I could only make out the product each of the merchant stands offered: food, poorly made weapons, clothing, and pottery. Maybe I could ask one of them if they knew anything? I needed to be careful though, asking the wrong person would probably be a death sentence. As we finally made our way into the center of the plaza, I whirled around, coming to a shocking revelation. There were no churches here, and no religious artifacts or symbols as far as I could see. It was strange, did Fortuna have no love for the Church either?

"Hey, come on, there's a pawn shop over there," Mars leaned in, almost shouting so I could hear her. I looked over to where she had mentioned, seeing another sign written in that unknown language again.

"You can read that?" I shouted back. She looked back at me, confused, then took one more look at the sign.

"Oh! Yeah! It's written in Yroni."

"You know how to read Yroni?"

"Well, yeah, it is my first language after all. My parents are both Yron." I had no idea. I remember being taught about the Yron people; they were the original inhabitants of this whole continent, sharing the land with the other native occupants, the Eidolons. That is, before modern society took over. There must be a larger population of them here. Maybe that's why there were no churches anywhere; they had been scrutinized by those in power as well. And the populace often had racially charged negative opinions on them. I never thought I'd meet one, let alone travel with one. That would explain her darker complexion.

I followed her over to the entrance, both of us stopping when we noticed the signs that had been crudely painted on pieces of driftwood. These, however, were in a language I could read. "NO SAGES" was the one that stood out to me. We gave each other a quick glance and pulled the sheet covering the open doorway aside. I was quickly met with a musty, unpleasant smell. The shelves were all lined with useless trinkets and odd items, most of which I doubt would serve anyone any purpose. At the back of the building behind a poorly made counter, however, was a rather brooding, large man, who crossed his arms when we walked in. I caught myself staring at him as Mars quickly strode past me, pulling the sword out of her belt and laying it on the uneven surface of the counter between them.

"I want to sell this," she said, her voice standing firm. He squinted at her for a moment, then at the sword, then back up at her.

"Where you get this?" he growled, keeping his arms crossed. Mars simply shrugged, then crossed her arms as well.

"You expect me to let a woman come in here, and demand I buy whatever she says?"

"It's a rather nice sword, yes? I imagine it would fetch quite a lot." They stared at each other for a couple of seconds, before he picked it up and turned it over, seemingly inspecting it.

"This is of the Church. But I will ask again, where you get this?" He pointed at the religious symbol etched near the bottom of the blade, holding it out toward us. Mars did not break eye contact and kept her arms crossed, not saying a word. I could feel the tension between them; it was very uncomfortable. I stepped forward hoping to try and ease the situation and not make matters worse for us. But before I could speak, Mars finally broke the silence, speaking in what I assumed was Yroni to the man. He uncrossed his arms and looked at her, shocked, before looking back down at the sword on the counter.

"Forgive me, I did not know we were of the same." He chuckled, looking almost relieved at the realization.

"My family suffered the same plight as so many of us."

"Yes, yes. Of course… I can offer you six silvers for it."

"Done," she quickly replied and snatched the silver he had placed on the counter and strode past me. I could tell she was angry. We both pushed past the sheet in the doorway and squinted at the blinding sunlight. I didn't realize how dark it was in there.

"You all right?" I walked in front to get into her line of sight.

"Yeah. I wish I didn't have to hide being a Sage, I wanted to throw that asshole through a wall."

"Really? Even though he was also Yroni?"

"Race has nothing to do with what kind of person you are, anyone can be shitty," she quickly replied, turning to look past me. I blinked a couple of times and turned as well to face the many merchants' stands around us.

"Well… let's find something to eat." I beckoned for her to follow me and led her to one of the food stands I had seen earlier. A kind looking elderly woman sat on a wooden stool behind it. She seemed to be the only one in this entire town that wasn't shouting. The food laid out in front of us looked delicious, and we each grabbed an apple and an ear of corn, one of each for Bastien as well. Mars snatched a dried piece of meat hanging from a hook, telling me that Otto was probably hungry too. It cost us all our silver, but it was a worthy investment in my opinion. After she bid us a good day, I stopped Mars and told her to wait.

"I actually need to ask you something." I turned to face the elderly Merchant once more. The kind aura she gave off made me think that she just might help us. She only looked up and met my gaze, not saying a word.

"We're actually looking for someone to give us information, do you know who would know about what goes on in this town?" She gave me a disappointed look and waited a couple of seconds before answering.

"Yes, that tavern at the edge of town. The bartenders hear and see everything." She pointed toward the large building in the distance, its large wooden sign hanging above the doorway on a set of chains. I gave a polite nod and saw Mars already heading in that direction. I didn't realize she had heard our conversation. As I turned, I could've sworn I saw the woman shaking her head at us. We walked side by side, taking our time as we devoured the food in our hands. Otto let out a meow and poked his head out of Mars's pack; I'm sure he smelled the meat that had been giving off a rather strong odor. We had our first lead, and it led us to this dingy tavern, The Winking Quail.

Chapter 9

The mud-plastered walls exposed their neglect the closer we got; cracks and missing chunks were becoming clearer. The wooden sign was swinging gently in the breeze, its creaking chains being both welcoming and ominous. A couple of patrons lingered near the entrance, huddled together and glancing over their patchy shoulders at us, but quickly giving us no mind. I had to wonder what kind of crowd this place attracted, and how welcoming they would be. The man running that pawn shop didn't exactly fill me with optimism. The tavern was run-down, but it still looked more established than the rest of this town. Maybe it was just because it had an actual door, through which we could see faint orange and yellow beams of light trickling through the slats of wood. The light shining through was signaling the sun had started to go down over the horizon. It took me by surprise; I hadn't realized it had already been an entire day.

We both stopped before pushing open the door and gave each other a quick glance. Nothing needed to be said; we knew what we had to do, and we had become in tandem with each other. I stepped forward out of the loose sand I had been walking through and onto the worn-down wood floor, pushing open the door with a loud creaking sound. I froze, I didn't like how loud that had been, and had fully expected the entire tavern to be staring at us. But... no, I don't even think anyone heard. The place looked packed, and the boisterous sound of patrons came flooding out. We quickly bolted inside, wanting to find a corner or some secluded area to scurry to out of sight. The sound of wooden tankards slammed against the tables and clacked together as several around us were saying cheers, but to what I could not tell, their drunken ramblings made sure of that. I saw Mars out of the corner of my eye doing the same thing I had been doing, trying to locate the supposed bartender that the old merchant told us about. I had expected to find some large bar against the wall, some clear indicator where they would be, but with the rowdy crowd around us, it was proving difficult.

A sharp elbow jabbed me in the arm, and I spun my head around to see Mars pointing at a man standing behind a larger table, several shelves behind him full of bottles. That must be the makeshift bar they had here, that had to be our man. With a hushed 'come on,' I followed her to try and make our way over to him, doing my best to avoid bumping into anyone. I'm sure at least one person here would fly into a drunken rage if I had accidentally spilled their drink, then I would have no choice but to get exposed defending myself. We caught a couple of glances as we were slinking past the tables and stools; I knew we stood out, we didn't exactly fit in.

"Excuse me," I said, nearly lunging to the table in order to get in front of another patron. The bartender looked over at me expectantly as he handed yet another tankard to obviously inebriated man. He didn't say anything, clearly waiting for me to tell him what sort of foul drink I wanted.

"We need to ask you a question," I leaned in, trying to be as quiet as possible so the others around me wouldn't hear.

"About…?" he finally answered, wiping the sweat off his gleaning bald head. The rag and his shirt looked soaked; he must have been having quite the workout serving this rowdy bunch. I took a deep breath, I didn't want to ask the question on the off chance he could be the wrong person to ask, but we didn't have a choice.

"What do you know about... Sages?" He quickly stood upright, looking almost shocked. He crossed his arms and stroked his mustache, studying me and Mars. I instantly regretted asking, I feared the negative outcome asking such a question would bring.

"What an interesting night this is turning out to be..." he mumbled, clearly not meant for anyone's ears, but I was leaning so far over his table I could still hear him. I still waited impatiently, holding my breath this entire time in anticipation.

"Well? What do you—" He put up finger in front of my face to shut me up.

"Quiet, not here. Just play along." I stared at him for a second and gave a hesitant nod while standing back upright. He quickly darted away from behind the bar and through the crowd. I noticed the man sitting on a stool next to where we were standing had been staring at me.

"Never thought I'd be sitting next to a couple of your kind," he finally said with a raspy voice, squinting as if to study us like a sort of specimen. Neither of our gazes broke from each other, neither blinking. His glazed over stare quickly shot over to Mars, looking her up and down. I tried to discreetly pull one of my sleeves up, trying to make my emotions flare up. I couldn't tell what he was planning on saying or doing, but if he was going to try something, I had to stop him somehow.

"Go back to your drink, this doesn't involve you, does it?" Mars stepped in front of me, I'm sure she saw my hand and knew what I was planning to do. The man gave her a confused glance, then turned to face the back wall again. He seemed to be thinking for a moment, and simply shrugged and went back to his drink.

She turned to face me after a moment and shot me a sharp glance. She didn't even have to speak; I knew what she was saying. "Be smarter." I shrugged at her, a half assed way of apologizing. A quick look around eased my suspicions, no one had seen that exchange. Or if they had, they didn't care. I couldn't imagine moments like that were uncommon here.

We walked back to the far wall and leaned up against it, trying to blend into our surroundings as much as possible.

"You need to calm down," Mars uttered at me, still scanning the room.

"I was just trying to protect you." It came out almost argumentative, but I felt as though I needed to defend myself.

"That's not the point, Sid. Were you just going to announce to everyone here who we are? What if—" She stopped herself, pinching the bridge of her nose and closing her eyes.

"It's just… Thank you. For looking out for me," she finally said after a deep sigh, still not looking in my direction. We stood there in silence for several more minutes, anxiously waiting for that mysterious bartender to return from wherever he had lumbered off to. I was getting restless, the rowdiness of the bystanders around us soon blended into just noise. Everyone seemed to be having a wonderful time here, but honestly, I couldn't tell if it was just being they were all inebriated and this was the only semblance of joy they had in their lives. I felt myself judging them but honestly, I was in no better position than whatever they were in.

But finally, and not a moment too soon, the bartender appeared again, beckoning us over to him from the other side of the building. We quickly jumped out of our corner and made our way through the drunks without a second thought.

"Here's your room for the night, please be gone by sunrise," he said in the most polite and friendly tone I had heard in days. I looked over the full table right next to us, all of them only gave us a quick glance and nothing else. Right, this was what he must have wanted us to play along with.

"Thank you." I nodded and walked through the back door he was holding out his hand toward. The door creaked loudly as it cracked open, and I was greeted with a musty smell. We quickly darted inside and closed the door behind us, hearing the rusted latch click. We spun around to observe the dusty room, old furniture and storage boxes were strewn everywhere. I pushed a broken chair out of the way as I made my way through. The shadows in here were overbearing, making it difficult to see anything at all.

"Really wish Bastien was here so she could light up this place so I could see a damn," I said to Mars behind me in a hushed voice.

"Yeah, I'm pretty useful sometimes, aren't I?" That wasn't Mars. I froze, and saw a figure lean forward out of the shadows in the far corner of the room. I couldn't believe my eyes, it was Bastien.

"You two are crap at investigating," she said, smiling. I'm sure she was relieved to see us as well.

"Bastien? How long have you been here?" Mars jumped forward, clearly excited.

"Fifteen minutes at least. I'm guessing you were led to the bartender as well?"

"Yeah, by an old woman running a food stall outside." She nodded at me, as if to imply she had a similar experience. Me and Mars found what seemed like the only two pieces of furniture still intact and pulled them forward so we could all sit together. Plumes of dust and cobwebs shot up whenever we did so.

"So, have you learned anything more? Like what's going to happen next?" I leaned forward, wanting to see if I could get as much information out of Bastien as possible. I didn't like the situation we were in. I was always one of those people who wanted to know exactly what I was getting myself into, I didn't like the unknown. She looked over at me and shrugged.

"All I know is that whatever this operation entails, it happens in this building… somehow." I gave a slow nod. Not really what I was hoping she'd say, but then again, I'm not sure what I expected either. This storage room almost seemed like a waiting area. Maybe he was hiding us in here until they closed, and the place was empty? I had no idea. I could tell the other two had that thought heavy on their mind as well, Bastien seemed to be deep in thought the entire time.

"Here you go, love." Mars had opened her pack she set on the ground, giving Otto a chance to look around, albeit hesitantly. She pulled off a small piece of the dried meat we had purchased earlier and held it in front of him. After a moment of curious sniffing, he grabbed it out of her hand and receded back inside her pack.

Chapter 10

"You two have any trouble?" asked Bastien, watching Otto's tail stick out of Mars's pack and flick around. Mars shot me a look, as if reprimanding me again. I looked away; I was already well aware of what I had done. Controlling my emotions was something I had never been very good at; it would definitely be a tough lesson to learn.

"Almost, but we're okay. Some guy nearly gave us a hard time in the bar." She didn't tell her about how I almost slipped up. If Mars gave me a hard time, Bastien would have called me an idiot for sure. I made eye contact with Mars and smiled, appreciating her covering for me. She smiled back. It was… captivating.

Time seemed to drag by, and it felt like we had been cooped up in this dusty back room for hours, making the most of it by talking about past experiences and hopes for our futures. I watched the sunlight filtering through the dirty window start to fade as the day started to end, which gave me a somber look at the current state of my life. Sure, one could argue we were living on borrowed time, but moments like these started to make it worthwhile, and I genuinely enjoyed their company.

I stood up from the hard wooden container I had been sitting on and stretched my arms into the air, letting out an audible groan. Shifting your weight twenty times on that thing can only do so much.

"Yeah, tell me about it." Bastien sighed, responding to my

groan. She was also showing visible discomfort on her chair.

"I'm going to get rock lung if we stay in all this dust too much longer." The semi-common sickness that had woven itself into our way of life in these lands. Rarely fatal, but nonetheless very unpleasant. I walked over to the door we had previously been ushered through, just for the sake of stretching my legs for once. I stepped over Otto who was now asleep on top of Mars's pack, with Mars herself leaning up against the wall with her arms crossed, zoning out as she stared at the floor. Reaching the door, I noticed the boisterous sounds of the bar had quieted down. No, it was silent. Had they closed? Is that why we had been waiting for so long?

"Hey, the bar, I don't think there's anyone—" I was interrupted by a loud *click* from the bookshelf in the corner behind Bastien. She jumped up to face it, knocking her chair over with a loud racket. Mars also snapped out of her daze and faced that direction, alarmed. It slowly cracked open and made a loud scraping sound as it swung open, revealing two men standing behind it at the top of some stairs, leading down into what looked like a cavern dug out of the earth. I recognized one of them, it was the bartender; he was holding a torch and quickly darting his gaze to each of us. The other was a stranger, large and brooding. He had a receding hairline and thick scruff across his face, he looked like he hadn't shaved in days. They both took one step out into our dusty abode, once more shooting gazes between us.

"Right, why you lot askin' about Sages?" the larger man in front boomed. He crossed his arms over his sleeveless tunic. The three of us shot looks at each other, as if trying to decide who should talk first. I stepped forward, ready to speak to them, but Bastien put her arm out toward me to stop me.

"Because we are Sages," she said, standing upright,

seemingly standing up to him. That seemed like a big risk she just took, outwardly admitting that. I took one more step closer to her and Mars, I still wasn't convinced we were in the right place or what these two men's intentions were.

"And who are you then?" the man asked Bastien.

"Does that matter? I just told you what we are." He looked her up and down, and then back to me and Mars, as if trying to find some tip-off to verify if she was telling the truth. I shot a look at the bartender behind him, who stood there in silence. Why was he there? It seemed like the other man was the one in charge.

"Prove it," he growled at her and once again looked at the rest of us. His challenge made us all blink in disbelief for a moment. Here? Now? What were we supposed to do? Bastien and I made eye contact, as if asking each other those very questions. It was Mars, however, who stepped toward the man, getting his attention.

"Fine, we will," she said calmly. The two men both looked at her with raised eyebrows as she held out one of her hands toward them. I didn't know what she had planned to do, all I could do was stand there with the same expression as them. But after a second, I saw it, a thin root was snaking its way up the dirt wall behind the bartender, and they were oblivious. It reached out and started wrapping around the flame of the torch.

"Hey! What—" The bartender turned and jumped backward, but not before the root squeezed the flame and snuffed it out, plunging everyone into darkness. There were some colorful words being said in the confusion.

"Relax." I heard Bastien's voice, and a bright white orb started glowing in her outstretched hand, brightly illuminating the room. Those two stopped and whirled around, staring at her in silence. After a couple of seconds of collecting themselves, the bartender managed to get the torch relit, and attempted to stand tall toward us again.

"Okay, fine. But what about 'im?'" He beckoned toward me.

"I'm clearly one of them. Why would I be here if I wasn't?" I could tell he wasn't the brightest, I was just using his flawed logic against him. He was clearly just an enforcer. The two looked at each other and mumbled something in hushed whispers before turning to face us.

"All right, but we must do something first." He reached back behind the back of the doorframe they walked through and dragged out a very dirty-looking burlap sack, and pulled out three metal collars. They had runes etched into them, and the metal was of a darker hue. I recognized it, they were made from Dimerium. My father had brought some home from the mines in my hometown. Apparently, it could suppress the powers of Sages if it came in contact with them, and I remember how often The Church would come and pay for wagons full of it before it was hauled away to who knows where. I jolted myself in front of my two companions.

"Wait, those are—"

"Dimerium, yes. You lot need to put these on to suppress yourselves."

"Like hell we are!" shouted Bastien from behind me.

"Listen to me, I'm sure you all know by now those 'Chosen' bastards from the Church can sense the likes of you from a mile away. We have an operation to run 'ere, we will not risk getting caught." He held them out, indicating we needed to let him clasp them around our necks, his glare digging deep into us.

"We'll take our chances without those on," Mars piped up.

"And risk the safety of everyone else we have in our protection? Forget it. If you really want to take your chances out in that shithole of a world, then be my guest. But I am assuming you all came 'ere for a reason, didn't you?" We all looked at each other, shaking our heads. He made a good point; we really didn't have anywhere else to go.

"I understand you three don't trust me, but I don't trust you lot neither. We're all taking chances 'ere."

"I don't like this, but…" Mars stepped forward, reluctantly pulling her hair up. Bastien followed suit, shaking her head, still giving the enforcer the meanest scowl I had ever seen. I knew I had to follow suit; I didn't have a chance if I left and tried to survive on my own. After a couple of choice words ran through my head, I stepped forward as well. After he had clasped the collars on them, he quickly snapped it around my neck as well. The overwhelming tingling sensation immediately hit me.

"What, no chains around our ankles?" I asked with sarcasm, indirectly telling him that I still didn't trust him. He looked back at me with an annoyed blink and scoffed. The enforcer beckoned for us to follow him down the carved-out tunnel of dirt. I took one more look at the others before I followed in step behind them. The bartender stepped to the side to let us pass, looking down at his feet and refusing to make eye contact. He looked… sad.

The dimly lit tunnel was so full of dust from us walking through it, I could almost choke. We all followed in step, with Bastien in front of me and Mars behind. It was a silent and eerie walk, no one was speaking a word. I almost knew the others were as tense as me. But something felt… off. I kept having these weird sensations as we walked. Sensations that would pass by me as we moved. There was a familiarity to it though, like how I felt at that bench in my hometown the other day…

After a while, we had reached a wooden door. He halted us and began fumbling at his huge ring of keys that kept jangling on his hip our entire walk. The frustrated mumbles grew louder as he was trying to remember which key fit the lock on the door, repeatedly failing. It bought me a moment to think though, about what I had been feeling... Was it the dead I was sensing? Why would I be sensing them? I remembered what I had said at the campfire, "I don't see them, unless I look." Wait, that's right! My father told me Dimerium suppresses our powers; he didn't say it nullifies them. Then maybe I can...

I closed my eyes, struggling to channel any ounce of strength in me. I could feel the collar growing tighter, the tingling somehow getting... louder. It quickly turned painful, but I couldn't stop; there had to be a reason I could feel them, as if they were reaching out. I had to keep trying. Clenching my teeth, I opened my eyes, and I saw them.

There were two women standing near the very doorway we were waiting to go through; one was looking at the ground, the other facing the wall. Their clothes were dirty, torn, and stained with blood. I could see injuries on them as well; one had a badly broken arm and shoulder, the other... half her face was exposing the bone underneath. I stepped back in shock at the sight of them; seeing them was causing me pain from the collar, but... I could still do it. One more observation of them made my stomach drop—their necks... They were wearing the very same collars we had on.

"Who did this to you?" I whispered to the specter looking down at the ground. She slowly looked up toward me, revealing the other half of her mutilated face.

"What's that, boy?" the man bellowed, looking back over his shoulder. I shook my head and apologized, waiting for him to turn back around to keep looking at the door. Finally, he did, and I darted my gaze back over to the woman. Except she wasn't looking at me anymore; she was pointing at the very man in front of us, leading us down this hallway.

Chapter 11

My stomach dropped, and my vision tunneled. I stared in horror as this man finally opened the wooden door in front of us and told us to keep moving. This wasn't right; none of this was. Why did he kill them back there? What did they do? Was this whole operation a lie? I shook my head in an attempt to clear my thoughts, causing the spirits around me to vanish. I felt exhausted, trying to siphon whatever power I could with this collar on was draining, like I was sucking for air through a straw. But it had been just enough, and now I had a clearer image of what was going on. I had to tell the others, somehow. And soon.

The dirt crunched underneath our feet as we once again fell in tow behind him, all of us silent. My eyes felt especially heavy now; all I wanted to do was lay down and sleep. Even my legs started to feel heavy. I understood now why these Dimerium collars were so sought after; they really wreaked havoc on you if you tried to channel any sort of power. I glanced at the key ring dangling off his belt. The keys to our collars were on there as well; I saw him slide them onto the ring when he clasped these damned things on us. My head was pounding but I had to devise something, anything. There was no way to tell how much longer we'd have until we reached our destination, wherever that may be.

"Where are we going?" I finally mustered up the courage to ask, breaking the silence and causing everyone to look at me.

"Somewhere safe."

"What does that mean?" He ignored me. I opened my mouth, ready to demand an answer from him, but quickly realized that I wasn't going to get anything substantial out of him. Bastien turned around and gave me a confused look. All I could do what look at our guide and shake my head at her. She responded by furrowing her brow and looking back ahead toward him. I hope she understood what I was trying to hint. I hated this feeling. Knowing that something wrong was going to happen and I couldn't do anything about it. I felt furious, agitated, tense. I looked back behind me, maybe I could run for it…

No. And leave Mars and Bastien behind? Don't be such a selfish idiot. I wanted to kick myself for the thought even crossing my mind.

"Please, go ahead," the man said softly, he had opened another door and was holding his arm out, letting us walk by. I had been so absorbed by fear and anger that I hadn't even realized we had reached another door. All three of us slowly walked through the doorway and found ourselves in a torch-lit room. Tables and stacks of crates lined the nearby wall. Another man I had never seen before sat reclined back in a chair, eyeing us up and down. And on the opposite end… Cells. Three of them. Two were empty. Three more doors were on the adjacent mud brick walls. The one we had just come through crashed shut as the man closed it behind us and picked up a large mace that had been lying on the wayside. We all jumped and stared at him; I could feel the anxiety from my companions as well.

"All right… all of you, into that cell," he boomed, pointing to the opposite wall, the cell door already open. Before any of us could object, he walked up and shoved me toward it, nearly making me fall. My god, he was strong. The other man at the table simply chuckled and uncrossed his arms, seemingly enjoying this show.

"Don't you dare touch him!" Mars shouted at him.

"You see this mace? Do you really think I've never used this before?" I grabbed Mars's arm at his threat. I knew we couldn't do anything against him, and it was becoming blaringly obvious he wouldn't hesitate to kill us. As we turned toward the cell, he ripped our packs off our backs.

"Hey!" Mars yelled as the man pulled Otto out by the scruff of his neck. He looked confused as the gray and white cat hissed at him.

"Get me one of them cages," he said to the other man, who stood up from his wooden chair. We all begrudgingly walked into the cell, its loud rusted hinges screeching loudly as he slammed it shut behind us and slid the lock shut. Mars watched angrily as the man took the now caged up Otto through a side door before remerging seconds later. I scowled at him, but he merely gave us one last look and laughed as he walked away, heading toward the other man as they exchanged a few words before he left out the side door.

"Idiots…" a voice mumbled in the cell next to us. Looking over, I saw a young girl sitting in the corner, her gray tunic was stained and one of her sleeves looked like it had been torn off. And a collar just like ours was around her neck. She couldn't have been more than twelve years old. She was obviously a sage as well.

"You're really not one to talk, either," I jabbed back. She looked up at me, her eyes filled with so much anger that it made me regret my choice of words. I was taken aback; the sclera of her eyes was black. And her ears… they were mostly covered by her hair, but the pointed ends were poking through. She was an Eidolon! I had only heard about them before, that they're the ones that taught humans how to control their powers when we first started developing them. They had powers as well, but theirs were… different than ours. Humanity used to have a close relationship with them, given that we knew what gratitude meant in many years past. I didn't think there were a lot of them left. I could see streaks of dried tears on her cheeks, her skin was so dark it made them stick out. I shook my head and sighed before sitting down against the back wall of our new enclosure. Mars had been standing behind me and walked up to the bars separating us from her.

"What's your name?" she asked the girl. But she didn't move or even acknowledge the question at first. Eventually, she slowly looked up.

"It doesn't matter."

"I'm Mars. I'm from Puerta Del Sol. Where are you from?" The girl looked back down, keeping her gaze fixated on the dirty ground.

"… Sparrow. My name is Sparrow," she finally muttered, shaking her head.

"Hi, Sparrow. You're one of us, aren't you?" Sparrow looked up at her, blinking a couple of times. Mars put her hand on the collar around her own neck, and Sparrow did the same in response before nodding. I felt like a jerk, I snapped at this girl and Mars was being kind to her despite everything. I sure could learn a lot from her.

"Hey! All of you, be quiet!" the man from the table yelled over at us.

"Shut up, asshole," Bastien snapped right back at him, causing him to stand up from the chair.

"A lady shouldn't be using that kind of language."

"Get fucked."

The man glared angrily at her, before eventually waving his arm dismissively and sitting back down.

"That's Sid next to me, and that bundle of joy is Bastien,"

Mars said, introducing us.

"You're so funny," Bastien said in response to her, still standing with her arms crossed.

"How long have you been here?" I asked her, attempting to make nice with how I had acted earlier toward her. She only shrugged, still not looking toward us. I let out a sigh as I leaned my head against the cold rock wall and closed my eyes. She obviously didn't want to talk, well, not to me anyway. Not that it mattered; we had found ourselves in probably the worst situation we'd been in since the start of our little journey. I had no idea what they wanted from us though, but if I had to guess, we were going to be ransomed or just flat out delivered to the Church, and they would collect their handsome rewards. I made one last futile attempt at pulling my collar off, only making the lock on the back rattle.

"There's really no point, we can't even use our powers to get them off," Bastien mumbled, watching me in my vain efforts.

"I could use mine a little bit, but…" She sat up, surprised.

"What?"

"Yeah, in the tunnel. It was painful but… I could siphon a tiny bit. Dimerium… it just suppresses our powers, not nullifies them." The other two looked at me, then at each other before Bastien held her hand out. A pained expression came across her face as her hand started to glow ever so faint. After a minute, she dropped her arm in a pained gasp, breathing heavily.

"You all should save your energy; you'll need it for what they have planned," Sparrow spoke up, still in the same position she had been in this whole time.

"… What do they have planned?" Mars responded. The girl finally looked up, making eye contact.

"This whole ruse they put on, saying they save or smuggle Sages? It's all lies. It's a slave trade. We're a prized commodity."

Chapter 12

I almost chuckled at how comically terrible our luck was becoming. A slave trade? There was a market for Sages? His whole façade was starting to unravel, and I wanted to kick myself for not realizing sooner that something was off, only when we were in that damned hallway. I scanned the room, seeing the other two in my cell with me looking like they were struck with dread. That guard was still leaning back in his chair and looked like he was dozing off. I guess he didn't care if we were talking now. But one feature I didn't take note of before was the banner hanging next to the side door that our 'friendly guide' disappeared through. It was solid black with a single red vine emerging from the left, blooming into a flower at the end. Was that their symbol? It was… an odd choice, considering.

The cold ground was actually a welcome change from the searing heat that we had experienced before out in the desert. Trying to find a comfortable position was already proving to be difficult as I shifted my weight countless times since I had sat down and leaned against the back wall. The other two also finally sat down, both seemingly lost deep in thought. It hadn't been said, but I think we all knew we were going to be here a while.

"I feel like such an idiot," Mars mumbled.

"We all willingly got led into this."

"But I was the first one to step forward… I was so naïve."

"You're just a trusting person. You want to believe that there is good in this world, right?" I spoke up. She looked over at me, surprised.

"Don't ever change. Me and Bastien will always be here for you if things go wrong." I mustered a smile, trying to give her some kind of comfort. I couldn't imagine what was going through her mind if she was blaming herself for this.

"... I hope Otto is okay," she said in a sad tone of voice, once more looking at the ground. I looked over at the opposite door they took him into, and if I'm honest, I was hoping the same.

"We'll get him back," Bastien said confidently, her eyes still closed as she sat back against the bars.

"After seeing what you're capable of, I'd be willing to say no one can stop you," she added on, looking at Mars and smiling. She must have been referring to when she saved her from the gallows. I wish I could have seen something like that, it must have been remarkable to witness. It was a comforting thought. Except with the obstacle of these collars on our situation was that much more difficult...

Time seemed to drag by, but eventually my eyes grew heavy and I somehow managed to fall asleep. I had no idea how long I was out, but a loud clanging sound rang through the room, making everyone jump awake. It was someone else this time, a different guard now. He was smacking a club against our bars to wake us up.

"All of you, up! It's time," he bellowed. We were all rubbing our eyes, looking around confused.

"Stand!" he bellowed once more, opening our cell door with his key. The thought crossed my mind, I could try to run for it, shove my way past him and we could all try to escape. The door was open, would it be that easy?

"Hold out your arms." He was holding shackles that were chained together. The thought of us taking a break for it quickly subsided, however. Even if we did escape, how would we defend ourselves? Who knows how many of them there were. The three of us were standing now but none of us were following his direction. He stood there waiting for us, clearly growing annoyed. I glared him down as he made eye contact with me; I wasn't about to let him command us around. As he turned to face me, I spat at the ground at his feet, a mistake I quickly regretted. Before I could even look back up, his club struck me on the side of my head, sending me stumbling and falling to my knees. My vision became blurry and tunneled, my ears rang. The pain kept throbbing intensely from where I heard the 'crack' of the club against my skull.

"Don't you dare touch him!" I heard Mars yell, which now sounded muffled through the ringing. He reaffirmed his demands once more, adding that we need to be alive, but it didn't matter how bad a shape he was in. Giving how he didn't hesitate to attack me; I believed every word of his threat. I sat there on my knees, clenching my teeth through the pain, my vision slowly returning. I think I had almost been knocked out.

"Get up," he said as he stood over me. I heard him clasping the shackles on the other two, I guess it was my turn. I wearily stood back up, and he grabbed my arms and clasped them around my wrists.

"Let's go, best not to keep him waiting." He tugged on my wrists first, making me lead our chain gang while following behind him. I staggered out of the cell, my legs seemingly learning how to walk again after sitting for so long. We quickly found ourselves through that same side door the other had passed through before, and inside a large back room with several tables and chairs, lit by an array of torchlit chandeliers. The most attention-grabbing detail, however, was the large wooden stage in the middle of the room. At first glance, I thought it might be some gallows, but it was too low for that, and there was nothing that resembled anything of the sort on it.

"All of you, up you go," the guard snapped, pointing toward the steps up to the stage. It seemed like we were going to be put on display. I hesitated for a moment, trying to muster up the strength to walk up the steps in front of me. My head was still pounding, and I felt weak, even nauseous from the blow. I glanced over one more time, only to see the impatient slaver glaring at me once more, gripping that club tight. With a deep breath I willed myself up the steps and wobbled onto the stage, the other two right behind me. Some of the wooden boards beneath us groaned as we stopped in the center, looking around once more. I watched the man who brought us in make his way over to one of the tables, where there stood another. His back was to us, and he wore a dark red hooded robe that was torn at his abdomen, with what looked like a black smock underneath and black leggings held down onto his legs with brown straps. The two exchanged a couple of words that I couldn't make out before the hooded figure turned to face us, revealing a black mask with only holes for the eyes, and a single red vine etched into the side. He observed us for a minute before striding over to where Bastien stood. He was tall, very tall, and he had an intimidating aura about him as he came closer.

He stopped in front of Bastien, looking her up and down with his hands behind his back.

"Yes… you'll do," he said in a soft and deep voice before moving on to Mars. She refused to make eye contact, looking over to the side as he observed her as well, giving only a confirming nod. It was with me, however, that his demeanor changed.

"Fascinating," he said, taking a step closer to me. He looked at me up and down but stopped once he saw my head.

"You're bleeding. Are you injured?" he asked me. I didn't realize I had been, but that would explain why the side of my head felt so hot. I didn't want to answer him, and instead just met his gaze, doing my best to glare at him.

"Who did this?" he asked again, still not breaking his gaze from mine.

"Who do you think?" I snapped, looking over at the slaver who stood by the table, waiting.

"*Ah*... I apologize. Sometimes, they can be... dramatic," he said in a deep, remorseful tone, looking back toward him. The man that struck me shot up straight, seemingly in fear of the masked man.

"Give him bandages to treat his wound."

"But he spat—"

"Now," he demanded; his growling voice sent chills down my spine.

"They will fetch a high price, return them to their cell as well." One last command before he strode off, disappearing behind the stage. I didn't dare turn around to look. I didn't know who he was, or what kind of power he held, but I could feel the presence he gave off, and it was terrifying. We were ordered to quickly get off the stage, once again led by this man back through the doorway we entered through. His voice was quivering now, he was clearly terrified as well.

"And *um*... here." He reached into his back pocket and handed me a crumpled-up roll of bandages as he unlocked our shackles in our cell. I simply nodded and he bolted out the door, locking it behind him.

"Here, let me." Mars grabbed the bandages out of my hand,

unrolling them and wrapping my head before tucking the loose end in to make it sturdy. I don't know if it was the wrappings or not, but it did feel instantly better.

"You all came back as well, huh?" Sparrow piped up, seemingly relieved as she stood and faced us.

"Does that not usually happen?" Bastien asked.

"No, you're the first I've seen, besides me. I think we're his prized collection now." I looked toward the banner that hung behind the guard table, realizing the symbol on it matched his mask.

"He must be the leader then. His mask is the same as these banners everywhere."

Chapter 13

I lay down on the stone floor, desperate to find a position that would relieve some of the pounding pain in my head. Granted, it was less severe than before, but it was still ever-present. I noticed my vision started to become dazed as well, as if my eyes didn't quite keep up with my body's movements. I claimed the far corner and sat down, resting my head against the cold wall. I wanted to just steady my breaths and close my eyes, hopefully get some sleep for once. I felt the warm embrace come over me. But of course, that was not to be. A drop of liquid splashed on my hand, causing me to open my eyes. Annoyed, I wiped it onto my sleeve and tried to make another attempt at dozing off. It dripped again, but on my arm this time. I looked up to see where it was coming from and saw a crack in the ceiling above me. It looked like water, but where would there be water? Is there a well nearby? But—

"—Sid!" I snapped back to reality, the white noise of my thoughts vanishing. Mars was facing me, attempting to get my attention.

"Come on," she said again. I looked around, noticing Bastien also standing, and behind her were two guards holding three individual shackles. How… how long was I out for? Where were they taking us now?

I slowly stood up, hoping to not get clobbered with a weapon again for being the last to rise. Just like last time, our wrists were clasped, and we were ordered to follow them. This time however, we went in the opposite direction, through a new door and another hallway, dimly lit with the same torches as everywhere else.

"Lex has taken a liking to you all," one of them said in a gravelly voice. I noticed Bastien's gaze shot up toward him, her eyes growing wide.

"Wait, what did you say?" she asked, her voice barely audible. Her question remained unanswered, but she still looked alarmed, even scared. Was it because of that name...? He clearly wasn't going to entertain anything we asked. So many unanswered questions swirled around in my head, it was becoming so frustrating. He stopped us before my frustration could build anymore, telling us to stand against the wall.

"One of you at a time," he ordered, beckoning toward the door we found ourselves at. Before I could react, he grabbed my shoulder and pushed me toward the door, indicating I was to be first. I stopped in front of the door, hesitating. I had no idea what was going to be behind here, but I knew it wasn't going to be anything good. I took one last look behind me, seeing my companions and the guards, who were glaring at me with their arms crossed. I had to go in; I didn't have much of a choice now. With one last deep breath, my hand turned the cold iron doorknob, and I slipped inside through the doorway.

I closed it behind me, the chains on my shackles rattling. I didn't want to turn around but... that smell. Was that... incense? It smelled lovely. My curiosity seemed to erase my fears as I slowly turned around, wondering what this place was. I expected to see some torture chambers, more prisoners, bodies even. But... no. There was a table with cushioned chairs on either side and shelves lined with books on both walls. It almost looked like an office of some kind. It was so well-kept together and tidy. And in the chair opposite of the table…

It was him, from earlier. That man with the mask that we deduced must be their leader. He was reclined in the chair, observing me, his hands folded on the table. I stared back. What the hell is going on? What is this?

"Please, have a seat," he spoke up, holding his hand out to the chair in front of me. I would be facing him, I felt like I was in the maw of the dragon. I didn't say a word, but slowly lumbered my way over before taking a seat. The damned chains made more noise against me. I never broke eye contact with him, but noticed on the table between us there were bread and… wine? Was all of this to indulge? I couldn't quite put my finger on it, but something about him… his presence… It was terrifying; and yet he was so… calm.

"Comfortable?" he asked in a low, inquisitive voice.

"No," I said with a snarky tone, raising my arms to show him the shackles I had around my wrists, before dropping them back down to my lap, intentionally making the chains rattle noisily.

"Those won't be necessary any longer," he replied, holding up a gloved hand from the table and giving a loud snap. I sat there confused, but a searing heat broke my stare, and I looked down. The shackles…! They were glowing bright orange! I lifted my arms off my legs in fear of being burned but… I couldn't feel anything, only the intense heat as they melted off my arms and sizzled into oblivion on the wooden floor beneath me. I could feel my eyes bulging out of my head, did he just do that with a snap of his finger?

"How did… Are you a…?" I stuttered, still trying to get my composure.

"Don't ask questions you already know the answer to," he replied firmly, before leaning back into his chair once more. I stared at him once more, again refusing to break eye contact. I don't know how I didn't notice before, but I could see his eyes through his mask... his irises were yellow. That couldn't have been a natural eye color that basically confirmed it. He's a sage as well.

"You must be hungry. Please, help yourself." I looked over once again at the array of breads and wine in front of me, it did look delicious, and I felt weak from how hungry I was.

"I assure you, if I was to take your life, it wouldn't be through the cowardly means of poison." I jumped; he must have noticed my hesitation. He's reading me like a book. He was right though, going through all of this just to snuff me out this way wouldn't make a lot of sense. I reluctantly reached my hand out and tore off a piece of bread before biting into it. It was just as delicious as it smelled, and it was still warm. I couldn't remember the last time I had warm bread.

"You may call me Lex. Or Lex of Rams if you're feeling dramatic. And what's your name?" I looked up at him. So, he was the one that Bastien seemed so terrified to hear. Why though? She must already know something. I replied to his question by shaking my head; I had no interest in telling him anything. He had a surprised look at my defiance for a moment, before he broke his gaze and turned to look at a nearby bookshelf.

"So, are you going to sell us to the Church and claim your reward?" I asked him, still glaring him down even though he was looking away.

"No." Just a simple response, it almost caught me off guard.

"Sages fetch a high price in faraway lands. You will be... indentured, but free of being hunted and maimed like you would here," he added on. So that's what this was? He was a slave trader. And he seemed like he believed what he was saying that indentured servitude was somehow better than this. I looked away once I saw him starting to turn his head back toward me.

"The three of you seem to be unique, their auras are something I have not felt before." I kept digging into the food, hardly paying him any mind.

"But when I came to you, there was nothing. No aura. It was… an empty void." I stopped eating at his latest remarks. Auras? Is that what I could sense from other Sages? The one back home that electrocuted that girl… Even Mars and Bastien. Was that what that terrifying presence was that I had been sensing from him as well? And what did he mean I had a… Void?

"You sure love to hear yourself talk," I said with my all-too-familiar snarky tone of voice. Before I could say anything else, a bright orange flash made me blink and I was hoisted into the air by my neck. I struggled to open my eyes, seeing Lex standing next to my knocked-over chair, his hand squeezing my neck and I tried to kick for something below me to try and stand on. How did he move so fast? It was like he just appeared next to me!

"Do not test my patience." I kept struggling, trying to me his glare, but my vision was so shaky from my labored breathing. Mercifully, he dropped me to the floor, and I pathetically fell onto my back, clutching my neck and gasping for air.

"We're done here. I trust you know your way out." I quickly stumbled to my feet and gave him one last look, as he did with me. I was pissed, but I had to just leave while I had the chance, so I reluctantly opened the door behind me and left. Mars and Bastien were still against the wall, their eyes grew wide as they saw me still breathing heavily.

"Right, let's go." One the guards grabbed my arm and pushed me in front of him, presumably leading me back to the cell. Looking back, I saw it was Mars's turn to enter that room to be interrogated, I hope she wouldn't tell him too much.

As I was thrown into our cell, I sat down once more against the back wall as the lock clicked loudly on the door. I touched my neck once more, feeling how sore it already was. Not before long, Mars showed up with the same guard, and he threw her in next to me. I jumped to my feet and was relieved to hear her experience was uneventful. I would have never forgiven him if something had happened to her.

What really caught us off guard, however, was Bastien. When she arrived, she looked terrified and didn't look up from the ground as she was ushered into our cell as well. Me and Mars looked at her expectantly.

"Fuck," she finally said, crossing her arms, still refusing to look at us.

"You know him, don't you?" I finally asked. Mars shot her gaze at me, surprised, then looked back at her. Bastien only gave me a nod before standing there in silence for another minute.

"My… my father knows him. I've only heard of him in passing but… from what I have heard, he's a monster with how powerful he is." She finally looked up at us, meeting our gaze.

"We have to get out of here."

Chapter 14

A somber mood enveloped us all, as if we were all coming to the realization of how serious Bastien's words were. Escape was the obvious plan from the beginning, but how were we supposed to do it? The biggest obstacle, obviously, was these damn collars we had on. Even if we managed to escape, what then? We couldn't defend ourselves, and I'm almost positive we would be endlessly hunted down. We had to think of something; the guards were gone so we finally had an opportunity to devise something, but we had to hurry. Who knew how long they would be absent.

"Even if we did escape, we wouldn't be able to muster up enough of our power to fight," I chimed in. I hated being the bearer of bad news, but it was more important to be realistic at this point. The other two didn't react, seemingly deep in thought as well.

"Wait... maybe I can..." Bastien mumbled to herself, but still loud enough to get mine and Mars's attention. You could almost see the idea come to her as her eyes lit up.

"You can what?" Mars finally asked, both of us still waiting impatiently for her to finish her thought.

"Maybe I can use my light to... to pick our locks. I can probably muster up enough to do it." Could she really do that? It was more of a plan than I could think of, and probably the only solid chance we had. We watched as Bastien struggled to manifest flickers of light into her hand, the bright shimmering swirling around her palm as she struggled to hold it steady into a solid form. She started shaking as we watched in anticipation. Finally, however, a tiny orb of light Mars and I both nodded in agreement, telling her to hurry. We watched as she clenched her teeth, making her hand glow faintly. Almost immediately though, she let out a pained grunt and dropped her shaking hand. I watched in silence as she breathed heavily, staring down at the ground.

"Okay… I… I think I can do it." I had no idea if she would actually be able to accomplish this, but all I could do at this point was desperately hope that she would succeed. The tension kept making me swivel my head back and forth; if a guard happened to come by and see what she was doing… I shuttered at the thought.

To my disbelief, I watched as she lifted up her hand again, it still shaking from before. The bright shimmers swirled around once more, and all the light she had gathered migrated to her index finger, then to the tip of it. She was managing to do it! Sweat dripped down the side of her face and her breathing became more and more labored; she was obviously in pain trying to do this.

"Okay… keep an eye out," she said in between gasps of air as the light extended into a small sliver, almost looking like some sort of lockpick. I jumped in front of her, attempting to make some sort of attempt to hide her in case one of those bastards happened to stroll through. I could hear her behind me fidgeting with the lock on her collar, with the occasional *dammit* she would mutter to herself.

"Are you doing all right?" I quietly asked. I tried my best not to sound impatient, but the anxiety building inside me was undeniable.

"Shut up and let me do this," she whispered back at me, the

metallic clinking was still going on. I looked over at Mars, who had resorted to pacing back and forth and constantly looking around. And at Sparrow, brushing her long curly hair out of her face, who was still sitting like she always had been but was intently watching Bastien. I'm sure she had been listening to everything we had been saying and looked just as invested as we were now.

"What's got you all so riled up now?" I froze. A guard's voice echoed throughout the room; it had come from behind me as I looked the other direction. I whirled around, he was coming through one of the doorways and looking intently at Mars pacing. No. No, no, no. This couldn't be happening; we just needed more time. We were so— *click*.

I heard it. I heard Bastien's lock click. Did she…? I spun around, the panic clearly showing in my eyes. She was still holding the back of her collar, breathing heavily. As she looked up at me and made eye contact, she nodded. A wave of relief flooded over me. I wanted to collapse and thank whatever divine being would listen. We got one but… now what? That guard was still watching us. Bastien was staring him down now, along with everyone else. She looked determined, like she was planning something.

"We need help," she said, pleadingly as she stood up and pushed me aside, walking toward the cell door. I saw her hand holding the collar in place on the back of her neck; the lock was gone. She must have already removed it as well. The guard took a step toward our cell, looking confused but not saying anything.

"Please, one of us is injured, you need to help us." She was up against the cell door now.

"What do you mean? What happened?" the guard finally responded, but still looked confused. He came up to the cell as well until he and Bastien were just opposite each other through the bars. I stood there, just as confused, wondering what the hell she was doing.

"I need those keys," she said with a cold tone, as she threw the collar off her neck and grabbed his face through the bars. He grabbed her arm in an attempt to fight her off, but it was too late. Blindingly bright beams of light erupted from every orifice on his head. I could see his expression; he was yelling, but no sound was coming out. It ended almost as soon as it started, and the light subsided into shimmering wisps that dissipated into the air. His eyes were… gone, almost as if they were burned away. Faint trails of smoke seeped out of his eyes, nose, ears, and mouth. He was clearly dead, turned into a horrifying husk. I felt sick, but I had to keep telling myself it's either us or them. As Bastien let go and his lifeless body hit the ground with a loud "thud," Bastien clenched her fists and her whole body glowed bright, the air in the room vibrated as I shielded my eyes.

"It feels so good to have that damned collar off!" she exclaimed, crouching down as reaching through the bars at his lifeless body. I stood there in shock, still trying to process everything I had seen. She managed to jiggle the key ring loose off his trousers and immediately started attempting each one of them on our door lock. Not before long, a loud click echoed through the room as our cell door swung open.

"Okay, come here, let's get that off," she said as she quickly went behind me to get my collar off as well. Not before long, I heard that satisfying click as my collar fell to my feet. I could instantly feel a rush of my strength come back, as an unnatural and welcome chill flooded my body. Bastien was right, this DID feel amazing. As she got Mars's collar off, she immediately grabbed the key ring and ran over to Sparrow's cell door as well, unlocking it and quickly removing her collar.

"Why are you helping me? You don't even know—"

"Be quiet, Sparrow, you're one of us. We're going to look out for you," Mars interjected, not letting her finish her thoughts. The young girl looked surprised but gave a nod as if to say thanks.

"We need to leave; we can probably get out the way we came in," I spoke up, pointing at the original door we came through. Maybe we could run back down that hallway and through the bar, back into Fortuna. I doubt it would be that easy, but it seemed like our only option.

"Wait!" Mars shouted as the rest of us started bolting toward the door. We spun around, confused as to why she was stopping us. Before any of us could ask, Mars bolted toward one of the side doors, grabbing the handle and nearly ripping it off its hinges as she swung it open. Of course! I had forgotten about Otto! We couldn't leave him!

"Where is my cat?" I heard her yelling, followed by a couple of confused male shouts. Almost instantly, a loud rumble exploded throughout the room, and the ground shook violently, making me stumble and almost fall. Large roots boomed and ripped out of the doorway she ran through, mixed with several loud yells that suddenly seemed to be snuffed out. There was an eerie silence among the three of us as we stared in disbelief at the size of these roots that had wrapped themselves around the nearly destroyed doorway. A trail of blood started running out and into the very room we were standing in. She just took them all out like it was nothing! Just how strong was she? I didn't realize I had been standing there gawking until I saw her duck under one of the gargantuan roots and step over the trail of blood. She brushed her hair out of her face and calmly strode toward us, holding Otto's cage in one of her hands. His whole body and tail were completely puffed up; he must have been just as shocked as the rest of us.

"Now we're ready."

Chapter 15

We bolted down the hallway from where we had originally come down, praying that we didn't run into any more trouble. I was almost certain that all the noise we had made caused some sort of investigation, and I had only hoped we would be long gone by then. I knew leaving the tavern wasn't the end; we had to get out of Fortuna. It seemed like everyone in this town was in on this whole operation. But where else would we go? We couldn't just wander blindly. I suppose we would get to that when the time arose.

The sound of all of our footsteps pounding in the dirt made this makeshift tunnel echo, and the dust being kicked up was suffocating. Mars had broken open Otto's cage near the door and left it behind, he was now sitting on her shoulder, doing quite the impressive balancing act to try and stay upright. Each of us seemingly took turns looking back over our shoulders as we ran, trying to catch any glimpse of someone pursuing us. There wasn't much to see; the dust cloud snuffed out any hope of seeing ten feet behind us. But regardless, we looked again and again.

I must have been getting erratic; my fatigue was setting in and my shoulder painfully hit one of the torches on the wall, sending it flying off its mount and tumbling on the dirt ground. I could feel the chill of my power still coursing through me, as if I had consciously been using it. The tingle of spirits passing by me as I ran was an all too familiar feeling. I didn't know why, but it also felt as if I had a plethora of it at my will. Was this because I tried to channel it while I had the collar on? That it broke some sort of ceiling with me? I could only speculate, and I didn't have the luxury to take a moment to ponder it. Whatever the reason, I welcomed it.

We must have been running for at least half an hour before we finally found ourselves before that all-too-familiar wooden staircase that led up to our holding room. After a brief pause, I pushed open the door, noticing it was unlocked. We all gave each other confused looks as we saw the room was empty. Why hadn't we run into any resistance? This was all turning out to be too easy. After everyone hurriedly bolted into the dusty storage room I closed the door behind them, but we all froze as we heard the rambunctious noises coming from the tavern just outside the room where we were. Was it open again? How were we going to sneak by everyone? We were covered in dust, panting, and exhausted. We would definitely stick out. Especially Sparrow. We all still had hoods we could attempt to hide our faces with, but she didn't. And on top of that, she was an Eidolon. If anyone saw her eyes, or her ears…

"We don't have time to wait and figure something else out, we have to go through," I said, turning to face everyone. I was willing to do anything to be able to escape, and the other's steely expressions said the same thing. I had been clinging onto the faint hope that all the patrons were too drunk, or there was too much going on that no one would pay us any mind and we could slip out like ghosts in the night. I put my ear against the door to try and judge how crowded it was, but to my surprise, it didn't sound like there were a lot of people. This was going to complicate things. So much for going unseen. Every fiber of my being was screaming at me not to, but I took a deep breath, gave everyone one last look, and pushed the door open.

The loud creaking hinges echoed throughout the wooden building, and we all bolted out into the open. I could see out one of the windows, it was nighttime, and the tavern had gone completely silent. The loud door clearly announced our arrival, and a dozen or so people were all staring at us, their drinks in hand, and weapons strewn across the tables.

"What the hell? It's those four from the cells!" One of the men stood up, and I recognized him; it was that man that led down that hallway from before! These must have all been slavers as well because they all jumped up and were grabbing their weapons and arming themselves.

"Sparrow, stay behind us." Bastien put her hand out, stepping in front of her.

"You were right, we're certainly going to have to go through," Mars said to me, moving to my side and holding her hands open at her side. I could see etchings of leaves starting to appear up her arms. I had to get ready as well; there was no escaping a fight now. I tried to channel the chill at my fingertips, and before I knew it, an eerie cold erupted throughout me. It had become so much... easier. Not only could I feel the tingle of spirits around me, but I could see their wisps. And... I could feel the slavers as well, like a faint glow in their chests. I could almost... grab them.

One of the slavers ran up to me, his axe cocked behind his head, ready to swing. Without thinking, I grabbed toward one of the wisps and pulled it, and a headless apparition of a man appeared before me, grabbing the slavers axe and throwing him to the side. It dissipated almost as soon as it appeared, but it was enough of a window for me. I reached out toward the glow in his chest, grabbed the first thing I sensed, and pulled. I heard him yell as he collapsed to the floor like a lifeless husk. This white essence was swirling around my hand. What did I just do? Was this… his spirit? This new power was intoxicating. Finally, I had a chance to defend myself, and I had been waiting for a long time to go ballistic. I opened my hands toward every wisp near me, pulling on them like a puppeteer, and forcing them to manifest and attack another group of the slavers.

I could feel another tug, like a thread that was attached to my hand. I looked down, it was as if the spirit swirling around my hand was attached to the lifeless body next to me. I reached out toward it, could I control him as well…? I focused and held out my hand, the thread growing stronger until it felt like a rope was wrapped around my fingers, and I pulled, lifting my hand up. The body next to me became engulfed in black smoke before it rose from the ground, shambling to its feet and facing me. His eyes looked empty; he really was dead. And now he was mine to control. Just like the spirits, I knew what I had to do, and commanded him to join the fray.

Flashes of light distracted me, snapping me out of my power-hungry trance. I whipped my head around, seeing Bastien having conjured a bow made entirely out of light, and was firing blinding arrows that he was manifesting at slavers who were charging her. She was a good shot, nearly all of them were hitting their marks, sending them tumbling to the ground. It was just like in the forest when I first met them.

"Enough of this!" Mars stepped forward, the tattoos of leaves and vines now completely covering her arms and neck, her eyes were glowing bright green. With a quick motion, she threw her hands up and the ground shook violently as a tree erupted from underneath the floorboards, destroying them and sending wood flying and crashing through the ceiling as well. Vines whipped out from the tree trunk and ensnared the left-over slavers before throwing them in every other direction. I dove and tackled Sparrow to the floor, attempting to shield her from the mayhem and flying debris.

After the yelling and crashing stopped, I opened my eyes, only to see the tavern nearly completely destroyed, bodies and broken furniture were strewn everywhere, and beautiful flowers had bloomed in every hole where the floorboards were destroyed. Mars stood in front of us, panting. The leaves that appeared over her body were receding back into her hands now. The eerie silence loomed over us as the tree stood beautifully in the center, its leaves rustling from the breeze as its canopy was exposed through the ceiling. I gave one look at Sparrow as we made eye contact to make sure she was okay and walked up to Mars, who seemed like she was still trying to reel herself back in.

"Wow, you really didn't hold ba—" I was interrupted by a pile of wood being moved on the far side of the tavern, and a large man in an apron emerged from underneath it, gasping for air. His head was bleeding, and he had many cuts covering his arms. It was the bartender, the same one who led us into this hell in the first place. Rage overcame me as I angrily stomped over to him, grabbing his stained tunic and pushing him against the floor.

"P-please… don't hurt me."

"Why shouldn't I? You sent us to our deaths!" I shouted, fully ready to exact swift justice on him.

"I didn't have a choice…!" His voice was breaking, I could tell he was on the verge of tears.

"What?" I asked, taken aback by his confession.

"My… my wife, she's sick, her memory is fading. I couldn't afford the herbs to halt it. But their leader… Lex. He approached me and offered to pay me with those herbs for her…" I stood up, letting go of his tunic. He was sobbing now, barely able to choke out the words to continue.

"He wanted to use my tavern... and I would look the other way." I clenched my teeth. I wanted so badly to hate this man, but...

"I'm sorry... I'm so sorry. I just didn't want her to forget me." I stood there, unable to understand what emotions I was feeling. Here I was, wanting to kill him a second ago, but now I had to look around myself and realize the destruction we had caused. We destroyed his tavern, his livelihood. Another collateral tragedy caused by being a Sage...

"Sid, let's go," Bastien said from the doorway to the outside. They didn't hear him, and they must have walked outside, out of earshot.

"I'm... sorry too." I clenched my fists and tried to offer whatever consolation I could. He didn't look at me, only continued sobbing as he lay on the floor. I ran out, wanting to escape from all of this.

"Shit!" Bastien shouted as we all saw it. Dozens of slavers were running toward us from down the alley. There were so many of them, and they were all armed.

"All of you, run. Let me handle this," an unfamiliar voice of a woman said calmly behind me. I whirled around expecting to see Sparrow, but in her place was a woman just as tall as me. It... it was Sparrow! It looked just like her! Except her hair was now a bright white and faded into a mist at the end. She strode past us and stood in front, all of us gawking in disbelief.

"What? No! you'll be killed!" Mars protested, reaching out to grab her arm, but to our shock, her hand slipped right through her, only leaving a misty trail before forming into an arm once more.

"Oh, don't worry. I have the moon with me," she responded

calmly, pointing upward to the crescent moon above our heads. We stared at her in confusion, not knowing what to say.

"I can't be killed at night." Before I could even think of what to say, one of the slavers reached her and swung his sword. My stomach dropped as it whisked through her body just like Mars's hand did.

"Come on!" Mars grabbed my hand, pulling me in the other direction. I watched in disbelief as Sparrow grabbed that slaver's neck and witnessed him age rapidly before falling to the ground, looking like he was now hundreds of years old and decrepit.

"That canyon! Hurry!" Bastien shouted in front of us, pointing toward the faint outline of canyon walls in the distance. I took one more look behind me, witnessing Sparrow grab another slaver, except he shrunk and collapsed into a heap of his clothing as an infant. Another one of Mars's strong tugs on my hand made me focus on the task at hand, and we bolted toward freedom.

Chapter 16

My feet were screaming at me as we ran, not stopping for any stumble or noise off in the distance. My chest was burning from running so much, and eventually, I started to have a metallic taste in my mouth. We kept moving for what seemed like hours, the soft sand under our feet making it even more difficult to keep moving at a fast pace. The dead trees and occasional boulder gave me some reprieve however as I was able to cling to them for a brief second, taking at least some weight off my legs. I kept looking back behind us, trying desperately to see in the darkness if we were being pursued. The looming canyon walls stood ominously as if we were some sort of cornered rodent. I never could distinguish anything that may seem like a threat, but that wasn't going to convince me we had escaped danger. I don't want to think about what would have happened if Sparrow hadn't stepped in…

Mercifully, we found a large enough boulder that we could all hide behind, and all decided to rest for a moment. I nearly fell trying to sit down, the sand felt harder than it looked as collapsed onto my back. Bastien stood above us, her hands on her head, trying to catch her breath. A gentle breeze trickled through my hair, making the half dead juniper tree next to us sway slightly. I finally had a moment to collect my thoughts, to think on what had just happened. The horror of my actions finally started to come to fruition. I had taken my first life… and I never thought twice about it. The thought made me feel sick. Was I becoming the monster that everyone else made us Sages out to be?

"I… I killed someone," I stuttered, trying to find some sort of reconciliation for what I had done.

"We did too, Sid," Mars responded, who was now laying on the ground as well and looking up into the sky.

"I know, but—"

"As long as we only do it in self-defense, or to those deserving, we shouldn't feel remorse," Bastien replied, cutting me off. I didn't say anything, I didn't even look at her.

"I'll never say sorry, because I'll never be free." She crouched down in front of me, clearly seeing how visibly upset I was. I looked up at her, surprised. The morning sun started shimmering over the canyon walls, its warmth flooding over me. I didn't realize how cold I had been. But she was right, we were delivered into a world that hated us just for being born.

"We'll never let you fall down a dark path. And you're not going to let us either, right?" Mars sat up and held out her pinky to me. I looked at her, she was smiling. The warmth of the sun complemented her perfectly, like a fire in the darkness. I nodded in agreement and took her pinky with my own. It was a promise. And unknowingly the most important one I had ever made.

"I hope Sparrow is okay… I still can't believe she could do that," I said, wanting to change the subject.

"Yeah… she's a longer stronger than she lets on, that's for sure." Another thirty minutes passed by as we recovered from our marathon, it felt good to finally have a moment to talk about nothing, attempting to not being anxious or fearing for our lives, even though the thought sat in the back of all our minds.

The moment was cut short, however. We all jumped up, alarmed. Someone was coming. We could hear their soft footsteps kicking the sand as they drew closer. I wasn't sure how much more I could fight, but I wasn't going to let my exhaustion stop me. I extended my arms, an aching pain radiating throughout my body. Surprisingly though, it wasn't a slaver that appeared from behind the boulder, but Sparrow.

"Why did you all run so far?" she asked, her oversized clothes dragging in the sand, black mist still wisping off her. She was a child again; the morning sunlight must have changed her back.

"Oh my god, you scared us!" Mars replied, clearly relieved.

"I did? It's just me."

"No, when you went to fight. We were worried sick about you."

"Oh. There really wasn't any reason to, was there?" She looked at the three of us, confused. I tried to observe her to see if she had any injuries, but she didn't. She wasn't lying, she really couldn't be killed at night.

"How did you even get imprisoned if you can do that?" I asked her, the question burning in my mind.

"Well, I can't do much during the day." She beckoned toward herself, showing her changed appearance. It was the obvious reason, and I felt like an idiot.

"They just saw an Eidolon and I guess thought I'd fetch a good price or something, I don't know."

"Speaking of, what brought you way out here? I don't think I've ever seen one of your kind this far south." Bastien stepped forward, asking the pointed question.

"I've been... looking for someone." She looked at the ground, clearly unsure of how much to reveal to us. She kicked the sand at her feet a couple of times.

"But... you're right, I am far from home. I grew up in Obeshcha."

"Obeshcha…?" I asked. I had never heard of that place. And upon looking at everyone else, it seemed like they hadn't either.

"Yes? Obeshcha." She looked around at us, seemingly shocked at our confusion.

"Wait, have you all really not heard of it?" We all gave each other confused looks and shrugged.

"It's… a settlement. Well… maybe a village by now. Far in the northern mountains. Although, I suppose it's a good thing you haven't heard of it, considering it's all Eidolons and Sages." We all looked at each other, shocked.

"Wait, it's a village full of people like us?" Mars stepped forward, nearly shouting. Sparrow simply nodded at her.

"How… how do you get there?" she asked again. I wanted to know as well; it seemed like a safe haven from the sound of it.

"I… don't remember," she said quietly, once more looking to the ground in shame. We didn't say anything, but instead gave each other another confused look.

"The more I use my powers at night, the less I remember about myself the next day. It's really a double-edged sword…" she quickly added on, trying to justify herself at the realization of all our confusion.

"Oh… well, at least we know it exists now, I suppose," Bastien replied, looking over at me and shrugging.

"I don't remember where, but I'm sure my brother does!" she exclaimed, the idea suddenly coming to her. We all looked over, now invested in what she had to say.

"That's… who I'm looking for. He vanished a while ago… he's one of the very few of us who were born without powers so I'm worried." She admitted her plans to us, probably realizing she had let the existence of her brother slip.

"Well… right now, we should keep going. I don't like the

110

idea of staying in one place for too long," Bastien replied, turning to face down the canyon once more. Me and Mars looked at each other begrudgingly. We were still exhausted, but we all knew we had to keep moving.

"Wait, can I come with you?" Sparrow jumped in front of her, stopping her in her tracks. She looked down at the young girl then turned to face us, seemingly asking for our opinion.

"Of course, you can. We all must look out for each other, don't we?" I stepped forward, smiling at her. She smiled and gave me a nod back. Bastien simply gave a shrug and continued to walk down the sandy path. Mars walked up to Sparrow and held out her hand for her to grab.

"This is Otto, by the way." She turned her shoulder to show the gray and white cat who had once more perched himself on her. Invigorated with a new direction, we set off behind Bastien.

Chapter 17

I usually hated the intense sunlight, but right now it was a reassuring feeling that just maybe, everything will be all right. I looked up toward the sky, watching a hawk circle overhead, it's head cocking from side to side looking for prey. The rest of group kept a steady pace in front of me, with Bastien leading, and the other two in tow behind her. My whole body ached, I was hungry, and sleep deprived; but nothing could dull my resolve now. I finally didn't feel worthless, like I could defend myself and those I cared about; a feeling I had been desperately searching for nearly my whole life. I knew there was more to my power, more of that ocean of black I could dive into... I just needed the bravery to do so.

"I think I know why this is called the Canyon of Chains," Sparrow said to Mars, their conversation finally snapping me out of my trance.

"This is where they transport their captives out, I'm pretty sure. Where we would've gone."

"Wait, this is the Canyon of Chains?" Mars exclaimed, surprised. Bastien and I stopped and turned toward her, surprised at her sudden change of tone.

"Then... Animas Core should be at the other end!" We all continued to give her confused looks, waiting for her to elaborate.

"I have a cousin who lives there, Enze, he'll help us!" She excitedly looked toward each of us. After telling Sparrow to come on, they walked past Bastien and started making their way down our continued path. I exchanged looks with the white-haired light user and we fell in tow behind them.

"Are you sure we can trust him?" Bastien asked her.

"Of course! He was one of the few in my family that I got along with really well." Bastien didn't respond, instead sticking her hands in the pockets of her trousers and looking away. I watched her for a moment, I could tell she looked uneasy.

"What is it?" I finally asked her, forcing her to communicate.

"I've had enough of 'family help.'"

"Not every family is bad, surely."

"Would yours make you feel any different than mine?" she snapped at me. I blinked at her, unsure how to respond. All I could do was look away. I hadn't even thought about them since I left; and even though I felt no remorse for leaving, I still wondered how they fared, or what happened. I will never forget that look that my sister gave me as I ran, why did she look happy?

"Sorry I... I should've watched what I was saying," she said softly, I looked over, her expression had changed, and she was looking at the ground now.

"No, you're right. My family and I weren't close. My home life was hell... I'm glad I got away from it." She didn't say anything, instead looking straight ahead at the two in front of us who were having a lively conversation.

"I guess we're not so different after all, are we?" I nudged her, trying to lighten the mood. She gave me a surprised look, followed by a smile and her shaking of her head.

"Yeah, well... I guess we've all got each other now," she finally responded. I wanted to know more about her life, I had a lot of questions about how she ended up here with us, especially being from the capital of Artessa. But I wasn't about to pry, it was obvious it was a touchy subject; in due time, I'm sure.

"It's really incredible what you're capable of doing." Mars quipped to Sparrow. The young girl looked up at her, seemingly caught off guard, then gave her a smile after a moment.

"Yeah, it is, I guess. I wish I could do it all the time, though."

"So then, if your age changes, how old are you really?" Sparrow looked away, seemingly pondering the question herself. I looked expectantly as well, waiting for her to answer. After a minute, however, she merely shrugged.

"I know we live a long time but... I don't actually know how old I am." It must be frustrating to not know so much about yourself, like where you're from or your age. I'm sure her power was responsible for that to at least some degree. Mars was right, it really was incredible, but are the costs of using it worth it? Maybe only in serious situations like we had found ourselves in.

"I'm still trying to wrap my head around why my father knows Lex..." Bastien spoke up after staying quiet behind us. The thought caught our attention as we all looked over at her.

"Does that mean he's involved with slavers somehow? Or does he not know...?" Her line of thought continued; seemingly unaware we were all staring at her.

"I'm sure it's just a misunderstanding, right?" Mars exclaimed, trying to snap her out of it. She looked up, surprised, then realized we were all looking at her.

"Yeah..." Bastien didn't sound convinced. And if I'm honest, it seemed too much of a coincidence to be a misunderstanding. There were seemingly too many moving pieces to try and wrap my head around, let alone the fallout of our actions.

"Why do humans do that?" Sparrow stopped and faced us. We all stopped and stared in response.

"Enslave, hurt each other. You're of the same blood, aren't

114

you? It's asinine," she added on.

"You're asking all the right questions, believe me," I replied. It was an age-old question, one that probably would never have a good enough answer. Growing up I was always taught that essentially being 'different' was to be feared. That whole mindset really started with the 'Summer of Grasses,' the year when The fever ravaged Sura. Sages were the first to be blamed, with The Church claiming they found the culprit behind it, a group of Sages they quickly dubbed the 'Buried.' Evidently one of them had the power of disease and decided to ravage the world. At least, that's how their story goes. The fallout, however, was arguably worse. Eidolons were immediately ostracized, since they originally showed us how to control our powers so many centuries ago. Racism ran rampant, and they were forced to flee to the far-flung corners of the world. If they fought back, I am almost positive they could've taken us down quickly. I always wondered why they didn't, how they were able to withhold the urge to rebel. Maybe that's just my human mind thinking that, after all.

"Finally…" I looked up, seeing what everyone was looking at. Just past the opening of the walls of rock were wooden buildings, some looking dilapidated and nestled in between trees. Several commoners in soot-stained clothing were making their way down dirt paths and darting past each other. This must be it, Animas Core.

"I hope he's well; I haven't seen him in quite some time," muttered Mars, suddenly sounding nervous. I looked back behind us, doing my due diligence of gazing back down the canyon for any sign of someone following us in the distance. We really didn't have another option, either to go forward or turn back.

"We've got to get moving, regardless," I spoke up, stepping

in front of everyone. One of the men in the town stopped and looked over at us, noticing our group in the distance. I could see from back here how dirty his face was from all the soot everywhere. Without another word being spoken, we pressed on.

Chapter 18

We cautiously made our way down the dirt embankment and into the quiet outskirts of the town. Our footsteps crunched on the fine gravel, quickly making our hopes of being quiet and unseen go out the window.

"Here, put this on. It's probably best not to stand out here." I took my hooded tunic off and handed it to Sparrow. She reluctantly accepted it after giving me and it a confused look.

"How does it fit?" I asked as she slung it over her shoulders and pulled the hood up.

"You need a bath." Her snarky tone was the only answer I was probably going to get as she took one sniff of a sleeve and dropped her arm back down. I felt it was a little uncalled for, but as long as it helped keep her hidden, it didn't matter. The others continued on, but I hung back and made one sly sniff at my underarm. Good lord, I really did need a bath. I probably could've taken the slavers out if I had just lifted my arms up. I caught up to my companions and once more, another man stopped and stared at us. He didn't speak, only darted his gaze in between us and finally rested on Sparrow as we walked past him. I gave him one sharp look as we made eye contact, making him turn and be on his way. This town had a strange feel to it. The stares we were getting didn't feel malicious, but I definitely did not feel welcome. I couldn't imagine they got many visitors; we were a pariah to them now.

Our crunching footsteps eventually gave way to softer,

squelching mud. The ground was soaked from what seemed like a runoff drain in the bordering hill that was emptying itself through the narrow walkways. As we all followed behind Mars, she suddenly stopped, facing one of the wooden buildings in the distance.

"Before we go in, he doesn't know... what I am." She turned to face us, talking in a hushed tone. The rest of us all looked at each other.

"Well, this will be an interesting conversation." Bastien chuckled to herself.

"Let me be the one to talk." I wanted to chuckle with Bastien but the serious look in Mars's eyes made me second guess myself. This was clearly very important to her, as was the rest of her family. It was almost a bizarre thing for me to see, given my past. The three of us let Mars walk up the wooden steps to the front door on her own. The building wasn't in great shape but looked better put together than most of the town behind us. I could feel more of the familiar stares boring into the back of my head. I didn't dare turn around so as to cause any sort of panic amongst them.

After some more hesitation and a deep sigh, she finally raised her fist and knocked on the wooden door twice. After a couple of seconds of holding our breath, the door swung open. A man with black hair and soot-stained clothes was in the doorway, a shocked expression immediately came over him.

"Oh my god, Mars!" he exclaimed as he pulled her in to hug her. She wrapped her arms around him as well.

"Hi..." Her voice was shaky.

"It's been so long, what a surpri—" He pulled back, his hands still on her arms.

"What... what's wrong?" He noticed the three of us standing

at the bottom of the steps, then looked back at her. I watched as his expression changed from elated to concerned when he saw her looking at the floor.

"Can we… can we come in?" Her voice still shaky, still refusing to look up at him.

"Yeah… of course." He gave us one more confused look as he stepped aside, allowing all of us to clamber inside his home. I hadn't known Mars for very long, but one of the first things I learned about her was how she didn't want to disappoint anyone; especially not her own family. I could tell even from a distance that she was terrified to tell him who she was, who we all were. It was painful to see her like this, and I knew I couldn't do anything about it. The four of us stood by the front door as he creaked it closed behind us, lowering a wooden plank across it to keep it shut.

"Please, make yourselves at home." He gestured toward some chairs that were placed against a table on the far side of the room. We each expressed our gratitude and gingerly sat down. The four of us gave the periodic glance over to Mars to see how she was holding up, but she still was only looking down at the table in front of her.

"So, *um*… Is everything okay?" Enze came up behind me, asking. We took up the only four chairs he had, so he had to resort to standing. We waited awkwardly for Mars to speak up, trying to honor her wishes of being the one to talk.

"Um… well…" I started to speak, the silence growing uncomfortably long.

"I need to tell you something Enze, something important," she finally spoke up in a shaky voice, turning to face him. I could see tears welling up in the bottom of her eyes as she was still trying to fight them back. He didn't say anything, just staring back at her with bated breath, as we all were.

"I'm… well, all of us…" Her voice trailed off.

"All of you… what?" he asked, giving the rest of us a quick glance.

"… We're Sages." He stood there in silence, staring at her. We all looked up at him, eager to see what kind of reaction he would have.

"Hold on…" he started.

"And we're all on the run, we're being hunted… not just by the Church, either."

"Wait—"

"And now we've made you an accomplice, but I swear we've had nowhere else to go—"

"Mars!" he shouted, making her and the rest of us jump and face him once more.

"Just… hold on a minute. You're a…?" He put his hand on the back of my chair, as if to keep his balance. Mars made eye contact with him and only nodded, one tear making its escape down her cheek. I hated this, how it was making her feel, and I know everyone else did too. He didn't say anything more, instead just looked down at his feet. I could hear his grip tightening on my chair. I jumped up and turned it toward him, it seemed like he needed a seat more than I right now. With a quick glance and a subtle nod, he sat down, putting his elbows on the table in front of him. I walked over to stand behind Mars, putting a hand on her shoulder. I know it probably wouldn't do much right now, but it was the least I could do to offer any sort of comfort to her.

"I had no idea… how long have you known?"

"When I was ten, I started to be able to do things that weren't normal. Only my parents knew, and we all agreed to keep it a secret… even from the rest of our family… I'm sorry."

"No, don't apologize. I don't blame you one bit." He was clearly still trying to process everything as he put his head in his hands and took a deep breath.

"We… believe slavers are also after us now, as well. We just escaped from Fortuna, and Mars wanted to come to you, so…" I spoke up, trying to give some sort of explanation to him for the direness of our situation. He gave me a shocked expression, and merely shook his head before returning his head to his hands.

"Okay… so… who are the rest of you, then?"

"I'm Sid."

"I'm… Bastien… Voltara." I had never heard her last name before. I'm surprised she even said it, even though it reluctantly came out. The name didn't mean anything to me, but Enze's head shot up.

"Wait, like Craven Voltara?" She merely gave a slow nod in response. We all jumped up, shocked. I knew her father was involved in the Church, but I had no idea he had reached the rank of 'Craven' amongst it. Enze sat back in his chair, still reeling from everything. I gave a glance over to Sparrow, who had been unusually quiet at the end of the table, her hood pulled down far over her face.

"Not to make things even worse for you, but…" she spoke up, slowly removing her hood and making eye contact with him, revealing her dark eyes.

"And you're a…? Mars, what the hell have you been doing since I saw you last?" He whirled his head around to look at his cousin once more.

"A lot, apparently… you're not mad?" She shrugged, seemingly surprised that he hasn't tried to report us.

"Of course not, but I—" He stopped himself and took a long, deep sigh.

"I share no love for the Church either, but there are a lot of devout followers who reside here. It's probably best you remain indoors." It seemed he was finally coming to his wits once more. His words were like a cold drink of water on a hot day. I almost expected to be kicked out, being welcomed in regardless was a wonderful change.

"I was just making food to start the day. I don't have much, but… I'm sure you're all hungry, aren't you?"

Chapter 19

Sitting down and eating with everyone was a warm escape, and everyone enjoyed themselves as we all talked the night away. Enze was nice enough to offer the back room for us to sleep in, and the four of us all laid our belongings down to make makeshift beds on the wooden floor. It was a snug fit in that room, but as long as we had a roof over our heads, we managed. I lay there restless, my mind still spinning from the events of today. I needed to relax, but the thought of someone else coming for us lingered in the back of my mind. I rolled over, facing Bastien next to me who had already seemed to be asleep. Mars and Sparrow were across the room, with Otto curled up on Mars's feet. I lay there for a frustrating amount of time, trying to find some way to drift away. I closed my eyes one last time and felt myself become enveloped.

I jumped awake, my eyes struggling to adjust. I couldn't see anything, just darkness. After blinking a couple of times and realizing my efforts were in vain, I sat up, water dripping off me and trickling onto the ground around me. Was I in... water? I jumped up to my feet, the splashing making more noise all around me and echoing in the void. The black liquid all around me was ankle-deep and gave off the faintest reflection. But I had seen this all before... hadn't I? This seemed familiar, which in turn made my stomach drop. This is... what I had dreamt of before. Where I fell through the ground and felt as if I should be drowning. Was this just a recurring dream...? I took a couple of steps, the liquid splashing as my feet cautiously chose where to step next. I looked around, once more trying to find any sort of object to see, but to avail. This place seemed… darker than last time. I vaguely remembered being able to see at least a little, but now… And if this was a dream, why was I fully aware? Fully conscious of my situation? This all felt so real.

I took a couple more steps as I tried to rack my brain for ways to escape. This liquid I was walking through kept distracting me; it felt like water, and yet I could've sworn I felt it start to wrap around my ankles for a brief moment before it retreated back. Dammit, if only I could see. This shallow black ocean felt cold, a familiar cold, at that.

I took just a couple more uneasy steps as I fumbled in the darkness, and I froze. I felt something… as if there was something here that I just realized, but I wasn't sure what. I couldn't see or hear anything, but an overwhelming fear and feeling of dread overcame me. I spun my head around, desperately trying to figure out what this was. I felt it behind me, then to my left, and then my right. I was trying to keep turning to face it, the black liquid making its usual echoing splashes at my feet. I couldn't take this feeling anymore.

"Stay away from me!" I yelled. My voice giving a resounding echo throughout this void. I stopped and waited anxiously, waited for something to happen, but nothing did. Regardless, I stood there semi-crouched, ready to either defend myself or make a run for it. After a couple of minutes, I stood back up, relieved that the only thing around me was silence. I turned around.

"Open the halls…" I froze. A low, unnerving voice spoke behind me, right where I had just been facing. It didn't sound like a person, but rather a dozen individuals all growling in unison. I forced myself to spin around, ready to face whatever that was, but yet again there was only that infuriating darkness. I opened my mouth to respond, but nothing came out. That all too familiar fear was preventing me from speaking.

"Open the halls." It was louder this time, and closer. It almost sounded... disembodied. I took a couple steps back, starting to panic as I couldn't think of a viable option right now. I had no idea how to escape, no idea where I was, and no idea what I was about to face. I backpedaled more before everything seemed to shake.

"OPEN THE HALLS." It boomed; my head started ringing. The amount of force behind its demand was shocking, and I stumbled. Before I could react, a long, decaying hand reached out from the darkness in front of me. I tried to leap back, but it had quickly grabbed my forearm, a painful cold radiating from it. I felt lightheaded and quickly started losing my balance. I only caught a glimpse of the hand, but it seemed to be formed by dozens of smaller hands, as if children's hands had morphed together like a school of fish to take this shape. My vision was fading, and as I was collapsing, I blacked out.

I gasped awake, shooting up into a sitting position. Sweat was drenching my body. I sat there, gasping for air as the realization slowly started coming back to me that I was back in Enze's house, with everyone still asleep around me. Well, except for Otto, who was in the corner batting at a moth as it fluttered around. I looked out the window, the sky was turning a pale pink and yellow; the sun was starting to rise. I put my head in my hands, trying to collect myself from that nightmare I just had. My right arm felt sore, I must have slept on it weirdly. I started rubbing it as I tried to think of why I kept having that recurring dream. But more happened this time, so it couldn't have just been the same dream again. But still, that place… where was that? Why did—

I froze as I finally looked down at my arm where I was rubbing it. There was a dark bruise, and it was in the shape of a hand. The exact shape of the one that grabbed me. I stared in disbelief, my mind blank as I tried to process what I was seeing.

"What's wrong?" I heard Mars ask in a tired tone. She was looking up at me, eyes half open.

"O-oh, sorry, just a bad dream." I quickly pulled my sleeve down to cover my arm. My gasping must have awakened her. She looked at me without saying anything, before turning her attention to the light trickling in from the window.

"I guess it's that time, anyways." She sat up, rubbing her eyes and giving a loud stretch and yawn. I looked over at Bastien and gave her a gentle shake to wake her. She gave me an annoyed look before grunting and turning over. Sparrow had already been awakened by Mars, and they were sitting up together.

"I don't want to be the bearer of bad news, but… now what?" I asked. We really didn't have a plan past finding Enze, and now that we were here…

"I know, I don't want to endanger him anymore as we already have. We can't stay here," Mars replied, looking over at the sheet that was hung over the doorway to act as a door.

"I want to rescue others… other Sages. We must. But… I think we need to become stronger for us to be able to do that effectively." Mars's resolve was starting to emanate from her. Bastien finally had woken up as she propped herself up on an elbow to listen.

"I think that differs from person to person, doesn't it? How each of us would achieve that," Bastien spoke up, her white hair being brushed out of her eyes by her free hand.

"You seem to need to be around a lot of death for you to really shine." She nudged me, although playfully, she was serious about it.

"Yeah... I can feel there's so much more I can do, but... It's like there's a ceiling or wall in my way," I replied, the bruise on my arm still haunting me in the back of my mind.

"Then... why don't you go to Remedy?" Sparrow spoke up. We all looked at her in surprise.

"I mean, if you need to be around death, I can't think of a more fitting place," she added on, shrugging. The small hamlet of Remedy was where the fever first broke out all those years ago before it ravaged the land. Supposedly, it's where the Buried enacted their plan to eradicate everyone. The entire hamlet had passed away as they had no hope of combating or curing the awful sickness. Now it just sat as a crumbling ghost town, a haunting reminder of the havoc that a Sage can really cause. No one wanted to try and resettle the area, for obvious reasons. I wasn't even sure if anyone had been back there in years.

"That's... Actually, not a bad idea," Mars replied, looking over at me, seemingly looking for my agreement. I sat there surprised still, and upon realizing everyone was looking at me, I hesitantly nodded in agreement. In all honesty, it was a very fitting place. Rumors were that the dead had never been buried, their decaying corpses littered the area as they were slowly retaken by nature. I remember growing up, I always exclaimed how unfair that sounded, but was always reprimanded, being told it was for the safety of others that none traveled there. It was ironic, really, that a place like that, where the hatred for Sages really started, would end up serving me as a boon all these years later.

Chapter 20

Packing our belongings felt bittersweet, the thought of voluntarily leaving a shelter to go out into the hostile world seemed bizarre to me. The morning dew wisped in through the open window with the breeze, making everything we touched damp. I felt uneasy about going to such a fabled location. But I knew that I could rely on the others, I trusted them.

Upon leaving the back room we had stayed in, we greeted good morning to Ezre who had just awoken as well. We told him our plans, and he looked at us in bewilderment.

"Remedy...? Why?" he finally asked once he realized we were serious. An awkward conversation ensued with me telling him about my powers, and why we thought this was best for me to grow.

"That cursed place is near that port though..." His voice trailed off as he lost himself in thought.

"What port?"

"Oh, sorry. It's just a rumor. A shipping port north of Remedy, smuggling people out to who knows where. A lot assume it's a slave trade, but no one actually knows." The three of us gave quick glances at each other.

"I'm not going to try and understand your situation, but... I wish you all the best," he added on, accepting that our situation was way over his head.

"Actually, if it's okay, I want to keep Otto here with you... just until we return." Me and Bastien looked surprised at Mars's request.

"I've already put him through enough as is. And if this proves dangerous, I want him out of harm's way."

"Oh, well, of course," Ezre replied, stepping forward to pet Otto who was already perched on her shoulder.

"It would be neat to have a cat around, not very many of you left, are there?" His calloused hands picked the cat up off her shoulder, talking to him in a soft voice. Mars looked visibly upset at leaving him behind, I even thought I saw her lip tremble at the sight of him with her cousin.

"Actually… I'm not coming, either!" Sparrow exclaimed from behind all of us. We all whirled around to face her, confused as to why she said that.

"I still need to look for my brother… I can't give that up."

"But… you'll be alone again," Mars protested.

"I know, but I need to do this," she rebutted, stepping toward us.

"Do you know where The Shattered Coast is?" she asked Ezre, looking past Mars.

"Oh, um, yes. If you walk west to the coast, you can follow that south. Should take you right to it. I believe it's about a day's journey."

Sparrow nodded, and quickly darted for the door. The three of us watched her walk past us. I wanted to reach out to stop her but forced myself not to. She opened the front door, revealing the misty dawn that awaited her.

"Thank you." She turned around, facing us once more. Her gaze darted between the three of us as she hesitated to leave.

"You were the first humans to be kind to me. I hope we see each other again," she added on, a sadness could be heard in her voice. Mars took a step toward her as if to attempt to halt her, but stopped as I held my arm out in front of her. And just like that, Sparrow departed and was quickly out of sight. Bastien looked toward the floor and sighed heavily.

"We should get going, too," she said, breaking the heavy silence that had befallen the home. We merely nodded and gave one last goodbye and thank you to Ezre before taking our steps down into the open world once more. We threw our hoods on quickly darted down the dirt path out of town. According to what Ezre told us, it would take about two days heading north for us to reach Remedy. The serene stillness of the landscape quickly gave way to foreboding evergreen trees to our left. I couldn't see how tall they really were as the fog covered the upper half of them. A peaceful melody of chirping birds fluttered around us, making this chilly morning bearable.

"She'll be okay. You know she can handle herself." Bastien started walking next to Mars, realizing how unusually quiet she had been.

"I know… and Otto will be fine too," she replied, basically giving herself a pep talk. After a seemingly endless hike, the fog was finally starting to lift. And I quickly realized that roaring sound I had been hearing was the ocean to our left. I had no idea we were this close to the coastline. Flocks of seagulls and a harem of seals were living their best lives down below as we walked upon the cliffs above the beach. The salty air greeted my senses and seemed to make a lot of my worries blow away with the breeze. Off in the distance, something caught my eye. I could've sworn I saw one of the massive rocks protruding out of the ocean move. I stopped and turned to face it, causing the other two to stop and look at me in confusion. Before I could explain myself, an enormous, gray, scaled head rose out of the water next to it, seaweed and flora covered it as massive amount of water rushed off the top.

"Oh my god, is that a Torgaia?" Bastien excitedly ran up next to me, looking at the same phenomenon I was. It had to have been. Enormous tortoises with shells that often got mistaken for entire islands. Which was easy to do since they often stayed immobile, allowing for all sorts of flora and fauna to grow on their massive, spiked shells. We watched in amazement as it blinked once then submerged its head once more, sending a massive wave roaring in every direction. I took a step back in shock, but thankfully we seemed to be high enough to not get swallowed by the sudden rush of water like the beach below.

I wish I could've stayed and watched; I had always had a love for wildlife. The now continuous crashing of the waves distracted me while we once more made our way for hours along our route. I pulled up my sleeve and looked at my bruise once more, its unnerving shape still sending chills across my body. I took one quick glance in front of me to make sure the others hadn't turned around to see and threw my sleeve down to cover it once more. To my dismay, a jagged mountain at the edge of the cliff forced us to turn inland, crossing over a large field and bringing us to the edge of more towering evergreens in the distance. The large trunks stood proudly all around us, and their height blocked out a lot of the sun, giving the forest floor an eerie darkness to it. The faint snapping of twigs and the rustling of branches above us served as the only break from the silence in this place.

"Are we even going the right way still?" I asked, starting to doubt my ability to keep track of our direction.

"We are," Mars quickly replied as she led the way.

"How do you know...?" She couldn't see the sun either, so her answer wasn't exactly assuring.

"I asked the trees." Of course, she did.

After several more hours had passed, we seemed to have come to the edge of the forest, only for me to find that the sun was setting. I hadn't realized it had been an entire day already. My decision to stop and make camp was thankfully well received, and we found a flat enough surface to make our makeshift beds once more. I was exhausted, but the fear of falling asleep had started to dwell on my mind. Mercifully, however, I quickly succumbed to my drowsiness.

I awoke with the morning sun beating down on me, warming my chilled body. I rubbed my eyes and looked around, elated that I was still in this world.

"Not long to remedy now, I'd imagine," Bastien said, seeing that I had awoken. She was already up and packing her belongings.

"What do you think that place will be like?" I asked.

"Probably nothing left, honestly." I sat there trying to contemplate what to expect, but decided it wouldn't do me any good, that I might as well get moving like the other two. After a good stretch, I got myself packed up and was once more following behind the others. The fog had once again returned to envelope the land around us, but thankfully we could see the faint light of the sun shining through so that we could stay on course. Another hour passed by as we descended and climbed various hills, the dirt path growing more and more overgrown, showing how abandoned it had become. It was strange, the farther we went along, the quieter the world became. Birds stopped chirping; we saw no wildlife. Even the wind stopped blowing. Before long, we saw it in the distance. Stone ruins. Rubble and one or two decaying wooden buildings. We all stopped and stared in disbelief. It was like seeing a mythical being, something no one was supposed to see. As we got closer, we noticed several decaying totems made from bones and wood on the edge of the hamlet, probably as a warning to stay away. I had to stop, I could feel so much pain and fear. There was such an overwhelming feeling swirling from this place. I closed my eyes and tried to listen.

So much noise. So many coughs, gasping. So much crying, so many people screaming for help. My head felt like it was going to explode. So many cries and gasps were growing silent, only to be followed by more pleas for help. I could smell so much blood. And smell so much decay. I couldn't move. This was created by a Sage… How could someone have this kind of power? I could hear so many lives being snuffed out, so many cries. There was so much coughing, so much screaming. My head was pounding, everything was so loud.

"… Sid!" I was being shaken by Bastien, making me open my eyes, the deafening misery suddenly stopping. My vision was so blurry, I wiped my eyes. I had been crying, my cheeks and neck were soaked with tears. The others looked at me, wondering what the hell was going on.

"This place… It's horrible."

"We don't have to do this if it's too much." Mars stepped in front of me.

"No. I must. I'm going."

"Then… we'll stay back. We'll check on you later," Bastien replied, taking her hand off my shoulder. I gave a nod and clenched my fists before striding away from them and into this hellscape.

Chapter 21

My steps slowed as the desecration loomed. My feet grew heavy, and I found myself nearly dragging my legs forward, a battle of wills that the oppressive feeling of this place brought down. A gentle breeze blew through the verdant green grass as it shimmered in the daylight, making a deceptively peaceful aura. It was bizarre to think about, that to any normal person this would just seem like another abandoned location; a relic of the past that stood as a lesson of regret and failure. To me, however, the silence and emptiness was deafening. Others would never know how populated this place once was; they would never know that they've never left.

I tried to steady my breaths as I took several more heavy steps past a couple decaying wooden buildings. I could feel the vibration of someone long departed to my left, sitting on the now-exposed second story that was looking out into the world. Moments like this made me question if I was blessed or cursed with these powers. What made me more fearful than anything was that the more I dove into the abyss and let myself become swallowed by my potential, I could feel my grasp barely hanging on as I embraced it more. I was worried I wouldn't be able to stop if I let go and lose myself. My power was frightening, but I was starting to love the night; the feeling of being unstoppable was intoxicating, and I wanted to feel it.

I stopped once I had reached what seemed like a crossroads in the center of these buildings. The now heavily overgrown paths barely resembled a street anymore. I looked around me, trying to discern if this was the best place to attempt to channel myself. Everything seemed to become still, even the wind. My entire body felt like it was vibrating, death had surrounded me. Yes, this was where I should begin. I wasn't sure what exactly I was supposed to do, but I had to try something.

The grass shone beautifully up at me as I looked down at my feet. I took one more deep breath and closed my eyes. I had to be careful as to try and keep myself in check, and not let too much flood out. The familiar cold came pouring out from my heart and flooded my body to the ends of my fingers. It had become easier and easier to channel myself. My whole body felt a chill as I reached out with my mind everywhere around me. I knew they were there, and they would answer me. After a minute, the air felt different. It felt… stagnant, like I was inside a crypt that had been sealed away for decades. I crinkled my nose, this was different. I had been able to animate the presence of one spirit before, but this feeling was… much more profound. Like chains were lifting off every inch of my body.

I didn't know what was happening, and I opened my eyes. I gasped, nearly yelling. There were hundreds… all of them surrounding me, staring at me. They were of all ages, all different facets of clothing, all displaying different abnormalities. Missing teeth, blood stains on their chins, vomit, tears. They were all completely motionless; not blinking, not speaking, just staring. Some only inches away from me. They didn't look semi-translucent as before, they looked as if they were real…

I stumbled back as the shock overwhelmed me, tripping on a rock and falling onto the ground with a quiet thud. I yelled as I fell. My eyes shut almost involuntarily, I didn't want to look, I didn't want to see what I had done, what I had summoned. I punched the ground in frustration. I knew I had to keep pushing myself, but seeing all of them... Why was I even doing this? Dammit, I was so scared. Dammit.

I jumped, I heard the rustling of clothing, I heard one of them move. My eyes shot open, expecting the worst. I was almost ready to just run, shoving my way through all of them. But... as I looked up, I was shocked. The one that had been inches in front of my face, the man with black, unkept hair wearing a torn tunic, he was bent down toward me... holding out his hand. His torn, stained tunic nearly falling off his shoulder. I lay there in disbelief, staring at this mutilated hand before I took one more look around at all the others. They were still staring but... it didn't feel malicious. Like they were waiting. Waiting for me. After hesitating for a moment, I grabbed the man's hand, his cold fingers wrapping around mine as I used him to pull myself up. I tried to calm myself down as I once more stood upon the departed; I had to become stronger, I had purpose now, people I cared about. The hundreds surrounding me looked on, I knew they were still spirits that I had managed to completely manifest into frighteningly realistic apparitions. I had raised the body of the dead before back in that tavern, perhaps...

Not yet, I needed to be able to manipulate multiple, even hordes of them. I reached my hand out toward a woman to my right; blood stained her chin as she stared back. I tried to clear my head as I tried to funnel my powers through my outstretched arm. My thoughts became singular, clear, and commanding. Before long, she also raised her right hand, obeying me. I succeeded without much hassle. And now...

Outstretching both arms, I tried grasping hold of as many souls as I could; but the more I connected to them, the cloudier my mind became. Closing my eyes to attempt to concentrate did me no good either; everyone I was entwining myself to, all their last thoughts and moments were running through my mind. I felt everything, even every emotion from their final moments. I wanted to let go as I didn't want to have to endure that pain and misery again, but I forced myself to continue. This must be the penance I must pay; if I desired to manipulate others' souls and remains, they would need to become a part of me—and I, them. I wanted to speak with them, tell them how sorry I was about their fates, how they were forgotten. But I wasn't here for that, I needed to grow, not be sympathetic to those already left behind. It was a cold-hearted state of mind, but I found solace in the thought of them helping fight against injustices that still plagued this world.

Grasping and clenching my hands into fists, I commanded them to walk north. My head felt like it was being ripped apart as I attempted to control so many of them, like my narrow stream of power was being stretched to its limits. Only one of them turned in the direction I wanted, a couple more simply turned their heads, the others… nothing. I relaxed my hands and put my hands on my knees, gasping for air. I hadn't realized I wasn't breathing and how tense I had been that whole time. Why couldn't I do this? It seemed like such a menial task. I stood back up and grabbed hold once more, attempting to command them.

Nothing.

Again.

A few looks.

Again.

Even less successful.

I threw my arms down once more, disgusted with myself. I had grown so frustrated, was this all I was capable of? Just some stupid parlor tricks? My mind felt frayed, and that stream of power I continued to channel felt jagged now, not smooth. I knew I had to be able to channel more, like something was impeding me.

Wait... I've had fleeting moments where I felt it, felt the seemingly endless ocean of potential inside me. Those moments scared me in the past, but... maybe I didn't have a choice now...

Silence soon was swept away by a welcome breeze, once more making the grass at my feet bend and flutter. It was almost like a sign of me having a realization. I was so hesitant as I tried to prepare myself for the unexpected. If I opened myself up, what would happen? Would I be able to control it? Or become swallowed up and lose myself? I had no way of knowing, and that frightened me. I had to, though. I had to at least try. With my heart pounding and every instinct yelling at me not to, I relaxed and tried to pull myself open, releasing yet another flood of chilled darkness coursing through me. It wasn't enough, but I could even feel it all around me, causing me to open my eyes. Black droplets were seeping out of the ground around me, slowly rising to my eye level like bubbles in a body of water. I felt my feet become covered as the dark liquid started swirling around my ankles. I've seen this before... It was that same ocean from my nightmares. That black void, was all that my power?

I could visualize what was impeding me, what I could best describe as a 'door' inside my mind, with the black liquid seeping through it. I knew what I had to do, and I knew I had to do it. With one last deep breath, I opened my palms to the ground, channeling everything I had into them. With fear ripping through me, I took one last deep breath and blasted it open.

Chapter 22

A surge erupted through me, and I felt my body become freezing. Every muscle and nerve in me felt as if it was about to explode. I wanted to yell, but mercifully the rush subsided, and I collapsed onto my chest, the cool grass pressing against my face. I was trying to catch my breath; it felt as if I hadn't been breathing for a long time. I looked over at my open palm, a black shimmer quickly cracked across it. I could feel it... The amount of strength in me now. I stood up, ready to test out what had happened to me. When I closed my eyes, I was shocked. There wasn't what I visualized as a narrow stream I had to siphon out of me, but it was just... darkness. And there was no end to it in sight. I had become drained before from channeling my ability consistently, but now I felt invigorated.

The dead stood around me, still facing me. I hadn't lost control of them yet. I didn't know how long I could keep this going, but I knew I didn't have any time to waste. I opened my palms once more and looked at all of them surrounding me. I attempted it again, commanding several of them to face north. Without hesitation, they did! I almost didn't think it would work as I nearly gasped. My hands still felt shaky as I tried to control a small group, but it was still progress. The amount of power I had didn't seem to be the issue, it was how I could control it. It was like a wild beast that I was struggling to tame; and it took nearly as much mental focus to keep it from overpowering me. I had to keep trying.

*

Hours had passed, and I continued to keep my abilities channeled through me. My arms were shaky and my legs felt wobbly; I had grown exhausted. Every command and motion became a struggle, but I forced myself to not let up, to keep going. Controlling individual spirits was easy enough, and I had finally managed to control groups of them with relative success. The thought of what the others were doing outside of this hamlet kept coming back to me. I wanted to stop; the exhaustion was starting to turn into pain. But I knew I couldn't, I had to keep going, for them. I dropped my hands to my knees, breathing heavily. My ears were ringing, my limbs hurt.

"Dammit… This isn't good enough…" I said to myself in frustration. Controlling a handful of the dead wasn't going to do me any good, they still fumbled around like puppets on strings when I had control. I'm not fully in control of this. Maybe if…

A realization rushed into my head. I had just been siphoning whatever power I needed, taking whatever small amounts from this black ocean piece by piece. I could feel it trying to break free, and I had been fighting it for hours and trying to keep it at bay. Maybe… I should let it out, let it consume me…

The thought made me hesitate; but perhaps it's what I was supposed to do… I felt as though I had no choice, and stood up, taking one more deep breath as I forced myself to proceed before I could second guess myself. I once again let my power flood out. I stopped holding it back, and before I could react, it flooded through me once more. The feeling of the darkness caused pain in every limb, and I felt it swirl and cover my mind and heart. I clenched my teeth, trying to hold myself together. Rather quickly though, I lost that battle, and started yelling as I felt my feet float off the ground. My arms and legs were being forced to extend, and after an excruciating minute of agony, I dropped back down to the ground, stumbling but catching myself. I gasped for air, which resulted in me coughing. I felt tears had been streaming down my face, and when I wiped them away with my hand, I was shocked at what I saw.

It was… blood. My tears were blood. And my hand… It was covered in a black and purple swirling mist. Wait, both of my hands were, and my legs as well. I could feel every living being around me, every bird that flew past, every insect. And I could see… the remains of the dead below me. In the ground, hundreds of remains felt like beacons all throughout this area. They were so deep, and so broken apart, but I could reach them. All the spirits around me as well, I felt all of them pulling on me. I had control over them all, every single one of them.

My heart was pounding, and with every heartbeat I could feel the chill of my newfound power coursing through me. It was overwhelming, but it was intoxicating. I stood upright, clenching my hands into fists. It had become so easy to channel now. No, this wasn't channeling anymore, it had become… me. I had to unleash what I had now.

The mist around my arms and legs grew darker and started to turn solid, covering my skin like paint as I built it up inside me. I outstretched my arms and opened my palms. Black clouds came swirling out from around me with a loud 'crack' and dissipated out into the distance. The ground around my feet rumbled for a moment. My arms started to become more covered, and I could feel the darkness creep upward. The remains of those around me, I reached out toward the ground and pulled on them. I could force them up, manipulate them, and reshape them. I grabbed several of the remains, causing the ground to tremble as they forced their way to the surface. I formed the remains together, and they burst out of the ground with a roar as all the bones and decay molded into the shape of a seven-foot-tall golem. Its fists of bone slammed into the ground, causing another tremble. Several of the spirits that had previously surrounded me dissipated, this must have been their bodies that they had been forced into. I stood in awe at my creation, and laughed with a grin at what I was able to do.

I can do more... I growled to myself, once more reaching toward more remains in the ground, shaping another bone golem with another "boom."

"More." Another golem, and another. The spirits were dissipating quickly around me. The black tendrils of my markings were now covering my torso and creeping up my neck. As I kept going, I could feel what could best be described as a ceiling, blocking me off. I growled in frustration as the tendrils started to cover my face. Why couldn't I keep going? Why was there another barrier in my way? I clenched my fists once and let out a yell of frustration, pulling and creating more golems around me, reaching at least a dozen.

My heart was pounding in my ears, and the black tendrils were snaking their way into the edges of my vision. My legs grew weak, and my head became cloudy. I struggled to keep my balance as I whirled around, my looming creations standing over me, as if awaiting instruction. The darkness quickly covered my eyesight completely, and I couldn't breathe. I reached out, trying to grasp at nothing, and collapsed.

Chapter 23

A cool morning dew rested on my face, sending a shiver through my body. For some reason, it took me a minute to realize I could move, and I took a refreshing breath that filled my lungs. Upon opening my eyes, I was surrounded by grass and trees. Was I... in a forest? I rolled over to face the sky, taken aback at how beautiful it all looked above me. The tree canopy rustled in the gentle warm breeze, their foliage covering most of the sky. I felt it should be dark on the forest floor where I was lying, but it wasn't. I was comfortable lying there, and I basked in my moment of peace as I closed my eyes once more. Everything was still, everything was calm. It was... serene.

I felt myself start to doze off, but before I could, a root snaked out of the ground from a nearby tree and shook my shoulder gently. I looked over, confused, but ultimately ignored it and closed my eyes once more. It shook my shoulder again, and I heard a faint voice. I couldn't make out what it said.

Once more, I was shaken.

I opened my eyes and jumped awake. I was lying on my back, with Mars crouched down next to me, her hand on my shoulder.

"Were you asleep?" she asked me. I looked at her, confused. Asleep? Was I just having a dream then? I shrugged and shook my head, and she responded with a concerned look.

"What the hell did you do here?" A familiar voice. I turned my head to see Bastien standing on top of a huge pile of bones. I sat up, shocked. It wasn't just a pile, but a ring nearly as tall as me, surrounding me. I remembered, my bone golems I created that were surrounding me... They must have collapsed as I passed out. I looked up at her to respond, her white hair let down and blowing in the wind.

"I... animated the dead. Controlled them. These bones... I created golems from their remains." I looked at both of them, fully expecting them to be shocked and horrified by my confession. Bastien uncrossed her arms and blinked a couple of times at me, before looking at the ring once more, eyes wide.

"That's... wow," she finally said. Mars had stood up and was looking all around her as well.

"I'm ready now, I think," I added on, shakily standing up and brushing the dirt off of me. Truth be told, the memory of me losing control and thirsting for more power was still fresh in my mind. I had pushed myself too far, and it had consumed me. There was no way for me to know if I would just lose consciousness every time I pushed myself that far, or if I had gotten lucky. I felt I could still accomplish more, go farther, but there still felt like a wall in my way.

"Yeah, I think we're ready too," Bastien replied, Mars giving a confirming nod.

"We really should get out of here though; if we heard all of your commotion, I'm sure others did as well." No arguments from me, I was eager to leave as well. This place became hell for so many people, and now had given me an unpleasant memory myself. I clambered over the ring of decaying bones and saw the carnage I had wrecked upon this place. The ground had been torn up and dirt spewed everywhere, from when I had manifested my creations no doubt. This must have been the commotion they heard.

We quickly fled inland away from the coast. We all came to the same conclusion that if anyone else was nearby, they would have used the same trail along the coastline that we had. After about an hour, we all stopped, and I looked back. Remedy had long disappeared over the hills we had scaled.

"What did you two do while I was in there?" I asked them, my body still aching from lying on the ground for who knows how long.

"We battled each other, of course," Bastien replied. Mars looked over at her, smiling. I swear I heard a snicker coming from her as well.

"And... did Mars win?" I seemed to catch on as to what transpired between them.

"Of course, she won!" Bastien replied, frustrated.

"You got some good hits in!" Mars piped up, still snickering at Bastien's annoyance.

"We fought in the damn forest, Mars. You knew you had the advantage from the start." She crossed her arms, becoming stand-offish toward her. Mars simply giggled and shrugged, which was met with a squinting glare.

"Nothing as exciting as you, it seems," Mars said, turning to me. It seemed she had decided to stop tormenting our friend.

"Yeah, but... I still feel like there is a barrier to my true potential. I'm not sure what I must do." They both looked at me, seemingly surprised at what I said. They had just seen the aftermath of what I had wrought, and now here I was telling them I could do more.

"Maybe... you're just too alive for your own powers," Mars finally said, chuckling at her own joke. I gave a small chuckle of my own and shrugged.

After a moment, we all confessed how exhausted we were,

with the long journey to this region and events following. We found a relatively flat area underneath a couple of trees and settled in for the night.

The sun had already set, and our makeshift fire was burning rather efficiently for everything being so damp. A lot of the bread and fruits we had packed to bring with us were quickly eaten, and while it wasn't exactly a glamorous feast, it tasted great all the same.

"So, what now?" I asked the others. They both looked at each other with a serious expression before turning to me.

"We talked about this before we... found you asleep," Bastien started.

"That harbor that Enze mentioned to us, where they smuggle slaves out... It should be to the north, if he was correct. We need to save others, and I think that's the perfect place to start." I looked at them both, surprised.

"We're taking the fight to them?" The other two nodded at my question, and I looked into the crackling flames before eventually agreeing to it myself. We talked some more about pointless topics before Bastien decided to call it a night and left our side to go and lie down on her bedroll. I felt tired as well, but I wasn't quite ready to call it a night. Neither was Mars, it seemed. She took one last bite out of a piece of bread she had been working on as she seemed in a trance at the flames in front of us.

I watched the reflection of the crackling fire in her eyes, the flames dancing and making them shimmer like dark geodes. She glanced up at me, breaking her gaze away from the spot on the ground where I'm sure Otto would have snuggled up against her. I quickly looked away, embarrassed she had caught me staring.

"What did you feel when you were there?" she asked softly.

"… Fear," I answered hesitantly. I wasn't ready to admit it to myself, but I had been afraid. My power was trying to take every opportunity to consume me, and when I let it… I lost control of who I was. I glanced over at her and met her gaze, but quickly turned away. I couldn't bear to look into her stare.

"Fear of where you were?" I shook my head and waited another moment before answering.

"No. Of myself. I let it envelope me, consume me… I felt powerless, cold… afraid." I felt pathetic even admitting that. We stayed silent for a moment; I could feel her still looking at me.

"Is that how you felt at home?" My eyes widened, and I blinked at her a couple of times, startled. I opened my mouth trying to respond, but nothing came out, just an incoherent stutter. I looked back at the flames, trying to fight back the urge to tear up. All I could do was nod slowly.

"It's okay."

"It's okay?" I responded, confused.

"We made a promise, remember? We wouldn't let anything happen to each other." She placed her hand on my chin, turned me to face her and smiled.

"I meant it. You'll always be safe with me." She laid her head on my shoulder, returning her gaze to the crackling embers once more. I wanted to sob and did my best to hold it back. I felt a single tear escape and roll down my cheek. I meant that promise too. I did feel safe with her. I believed her.

Chapter 24

We all slept soundly that night. The loose dirt underneath us proved to make a comfortable bed once you positioned yourself correctly. I stretched and let out an audible groan as I opened my eyes, disappointed that I had already forgotten the pleasant dream I was having. It was still nighttime, to my surprise. I thought that was odd, considering I felt so well-rested.

"I see you're not the only one up at a strange hour," Bastien said to me. She must have seen me looking up at the night sky.

"Yeah, I guess so. The sun must be coming up any minute now," I replied, brushing it off and rising to my feet. I looked over next to me to see an empty bedroll where Mars had been sleeping.

"She said she had to go 'commune' with the plants, or something," Bastien answered my inquisitive looking around, shrugging. I didn't reply and merely gave a glance into the trees, but quickly decided I had best try and help by packing everything up. Almost immediately, however, I heard Mars walking back toward us as I was rolling my blanket back up. She had her arms crossed and was looking down at her feet as she walked, lost in thought.

"You going to be ready to go?" Bastien asked her, looking up and stopping what she was doing.

"Yeah…" she replied, looking up at the sky, still seemingly distracted. I made eye contact with Bastien as we were both seemingly asking what had gotten into her.

"What is it?" I asked, trying to get her to come back to reality.

"Oh, sorry. It's nothing." She quickly knelt down and started packing up her belongings as well. After a while, we were ready to go and looked around us to try and get our bearings in the darkness. We didn't have a trail to follow anymore, just the sun to guide us in which direction we needed to go. With it being nighttime, however, that was proving rather difficult.

"The tree line was going to be to our right, so that's as good as we've got now," Bastien spoke up, holding out her hand and creating a small orb of light that brightened the area around us like a torch. We followed her as we slowly made our way through bushes and large rocks that dotted the landscape. The shadows being cast off her hand that were bouncing off every object around us would make even the bravest adventurer look twice.

"Why can't I find the moon anywhere?" Mars asked herself, and I turned around to find her looking up at the sky once more. I found myself starting to look up as well, and I didn't see any sign of it either. In fact, there were not even any stars.

"It must be cloudy." My best reason I could think of. It seemed plausible; however, I couldn't shake the weird feeling I had that so much time had passed since we all had awakened, and there was still no light on the horizon from the morning sun. It must have been earlier in the night than I had thought. I got no response from her, and she simply strode past me. The landscape seemed to blend together as we pushed on, the light in Bastien's hand never wavering. I was quickly realizing how grateful I was to have someone like her with us. I had no way to tell how long we had been walking, the only distinctive landmarks were the edge of the forest curving and changing direction every so often.

"Wait." Mars suddenly stopped, grabbing Bastien's arm.

She stopped and turned around, confused. The light in her hand now making me squint.

"We're being followed."

"What—"

"Since we left Animas Core, we've been followed."

I looked confused, then turned around to look into the darkness, trying to see what Mars was talking about.

"How do you know we're being followed?" I turned back toward her to ask. I hadn't heard, seen, or sensed anything. Just the occasional wildlife scampering around or flying away.

"The plants speak to me; they've been telling me."

I responded by looking behind me again, wondering who would have been determined enough to follow us for this long. Maybe someone recognized us back in that town, or maybe they realized what we were.

"They've been stepping in the exact same spots as us, as if mimicking us. I've sensed us three taking steps, then after a while, a fourth."

"If we're being followed, why are you just now telling us?" Bastien stepped toward her, annoyed.

"The steps are so light, I assumed it was just an animal following our scent. But they're quickly growing closer to us, it's all too intentional." Her words sent a chill down my spine. I didn't like how this sounded. Bastien quickly extinguished her orb of light, and we were once more enveloped in darkness. I held myself back from trying to manifest my powers on the off chance that it was a Sage, they would sense me if I did. We all stood tense, listening to the deafening silence around us.

"Are they still moving…?" Bastien whispered.

"No, but…"

"But what?"

"They stopped moving… but they're not standing anywhere either. I'm asking but only being told there's no one." Mars knelt down and put her hand on the grass at her feet, taking a deep breath. I watched her stay motionless and silent before I looked back at the tree once more. I wasn't sure what to expect but was hoping I'd only see a deer or something else harmless.

"That's strange… they seem to be gone now," Mars said in a defeated tone of voice, rising to her feet.

"Well, keep listening, maybe they're still around." Bastien turned back toward our original path, ready to create an orb of light once more.

"Maybe it was—"

"Wait!" Mars stopped me mid-sentence, shouting as she whirled toward the trees on our right.

"Over there!" She pointed, and I squinted to see what she was aiming at. Once I saw it, I felt my blood run cold. There were eyes; just white, blank eyes seemingly staring at us from deep in the forest. An arrow of light went flying past us with a loud 'crack' and impaled itself in the tree next to where Mars had been pointing. Bastien opened her hand and the arrow illuminated brightly, revealing the area. There was no one, still just the pale white eyes, floating in the air. We stood in disbelief for a brief moment.

"What the hell is—" I was cut off but a loud 'whoosh' as they burst into three plumes of gray smoke and rapidly flew into the sky above us, making the nearby trees bend and sway. Gusts of wind boomed out toward us as they kept climbing higher into the sky, swirling around each other. As we stared upward, they changed direction and started free falling down toward us. I stumbled backward, doing my best to gauge where they were headed. As they got closer, however, it became clear, they were splitting up toward all three of us. At the last moment, I dove out of the way as one of the plumes crashed into the ground, the smoke flying out in every direction. The other two crashed by my companions as well, and I quickly jumped to my feet ready to defend myself from whatever this was.

To my surprise, I saw a woman clad in monk's clothing standing where the smoke had crashed into the ground. She was looking at the ground, her fingers interlaced together. I glanced over and saw that with the others, there were actually three women, and they looked exactly the same. Their pure white eyes were sunken back into their skulls, and their skin was showing signs of age with wrinkles near the eyes and cheeks. She slowly raised her head to look at me, and I froze. I could sense her now, an overwhelming choking feeling in my throat. She was clearly a Sage. I heard a yell coming from my right, the woman that landed near Bastien had already engaged her.

A sudden movement made me whip my head back around, the woman in front of me was lunging at me now, a curved blade protruding from her sleeve.

Chapter 25

The sight of the blade made me freeze, and I watched as the world slowed around me. I didn't have enough time to defend myself, and I wasn't sure if I could dive out of the way in time. I stumbled backward before I heard a loud rumble, and I barely had time to look over to my right before a large root tore up through the ground, striking me and sending me flying to the ground. I crashed and tumbled with a loud thud as I saw the woman's blade become impaled in the now motionless root.

"You need to watch yourself!" I heard Mars yell. I looked over to where she yelled from, seeing her dealing with her own duplicate of this woman, all the while shooting me a serious look. Her hair had already become undone from being tied up, and the left side of her clothes were covered in dirt. She must have already been knocked down, and she was losing ground. She still watched out for me, saved me. The robed woman let out a frustrated growl before ripping her blade out of the root before turning toward my general direction.

"And will you not fight back?" she hissed, clutching the edge of the weapon once more. I lay there motionless, waiting to be attacked again, but she just stood there. Did she… not know where I was? Was she blind?

I slowly rose to my feet, not taking my eyes off her. She still stayed motionless, waiting. This must be my chance, if she couldn't see me, I could channel my powers and… no, wait. That must be how she can 'see' us. If I channeled my powers, she'd sense me, and attack. That must be how she's been fighting the other two.

I looked over at Bastien, trying to gauge how well she was holding her own. A blinding staff of light came whipping out and ripped through pillars of smoke as they'd reform into that woman, before quickly being struck through by Bastien over and over. I heard her yell an obscenity before I saw her being thrown back and landing on her shoulder, sliding a couple of feet through the grass. The duplicate she had been fighting stood there with an outstretched palm as the smoke settled around her, seemingly unfazed by Bastien's attacks. I didn't want to channel my powers, especially if I had to fight someone who I could only guess what they were capable of. But seeing how the others were fairing, I didn't have a choice.

I took a couple of steps back to try and give myself some more room before I opened my palms and clenched my teeth. I tried to not let all of it come flooding out, lest I lose control again. The all-too-familiar chill coursed through my hands and up my arms, and I saw the black mist return as it tightly wound around my fingers. The woman's head whipped toward me, and was immediately running toward me, blade in hand. I didn't expect her to sense me so fast, and I quickly tried to think of some way to defend myself. As I was about to attempt to channel something, I saw a faint glow underneath me, there were remains underneath us, bones. They felt like… animal remains. I glanced back up; she was nearly to me. I panicked and reached out toward the remains, pulling them toward me without any thought in my mind. As she lunged with her arm cocked back, the remains below me burst from the ground, forming around my hand and forearm into a blade made of bone. Without a second to spare, I threw my arm up, deflecting her dagger away from me with a loud 'clang.' We both stumbled, and I threw my arm out toward her, sending the bones flying off me and through her like dozens of projectiles. They pierced her body clean through, sending out plumes of smoke behind her before she eventually burst into a cloud and reformed tens of feet away from me. I stood back up, trying to catch my breath and frantically thinking of just how I was supposed to fight her.

I was fully expecting her to attack me again, but she didn't. She merely looked at me and smiled.

"Now you'll see what I see," she cackled, reaching her arm into the sky. I looked up confused, and felt my stomach drop as I saw the darkness of the sky bubble and writhe above me. I looked at the others, all the duplicates were doing the same thing, my companions looking up horrified as well. Before I could shout at them, I heard a loud rushing sound like a raging river. The night sky came crashing down on us, crushing me into the ground and causing all the air to escape from my lungs. I couldn't yell, just opened my mouth desperate to catch a breath of air under the crushing weight. Rather quickly though, it lifted, and the deafening roar of the night sky was gone. I opened my eyes, but it was still dark. Shockingly dark, in fact. I pushed myself up, trying to get my eyes to adjust, but to no avail. Did she make the night darker? No, something was wrong. I could feel the sunlight kissing my skin, its warmth radiating over my face. The sun was out. I felt my face… the night sky, it was covering my eyes. I frantically tried to rub it off, but no matter how hard I clawed at it, it wouldn't budge. She blinded me. And it wasn't nighttime at all, that must have been her this entire time. She changed the whole sky…

I heard her laugh as I whirled around, trying to hear where she was standing. It seemed to be coming from all around me, like there were dozens of her. I held my hand out, trying to see if I could sense her soul or anything at all, but an overwhelming force slammed into my side, sending me flying off my feet for at least a couple of seconds before slamming once more into the ground. The pain on my side shot throughout my body, I felt like I had just gotten hit by a raging bull. Smoke burned my nostrils and throat, making me cough as I tried to wheeze and catch my breath. Once more I held out my hand, trying to focus in between breaths, desperately searching for someone's soul as a marker that I could use. Again, I was slammed into the air and crashed into the ground, the force making me yell out in pain. I was screwed, she was going to beat me until she killed me unless I could think of something to do. The pain shot through my shoulder as I tried to lift my arm once more, causing me to recoil.

I tried once more but heard a loud yell that caused me to freeze. It sounded like Bastien, and the yell didn't stop. I shuddered at the thought of what was being done to her.

"Hang on! I'm coming!" I yelled as I forced myself onto my feet, my legs wobbling underneath me. It was an empty exclamation, I had no idea what I could actually do, but I had to at least try. I only got about two steps in before a bright light started burning through the darkness on my eyes, steadily revealing the bright day-lit world around me. That's when I realized, she wasn't in pain, she was channeling everything she had to burn this darkness away. Her yelling continued, barely taking a breath before starting once more. I squinted as the darkness seemingly dissolved off of me and was in disbelief as I saw her. I could only make out a silhouette of her body as she shone brighter than the sun. The women in the monk robes recoiled, seemingly surprised by what was happening. Finally, the yelling ceased, and she collapsed to her knees. Her body stopped glowing so fiercely, but her hair looked like it had turned into light themselves, giving off their own individual glow.

I stood there clutching one of my arms, the pain still throbbing after being thrown around as our attackers all burst into plumes of smoke, merging into one as they ascended quickly into the sky before arching back down and crashing into the ground near the forest's edge. The singular woman appeared once more.

"The Daughters will be pleased," she said to us as she looked over her shoulder. Bastien let out one more yell as she fired another arrow of light toward her, but she evaporated into thin air as the arrow struck a tree before evaporating itself.

"Dammit!" Bastien yelled as she breathed heavily, her hair starting to return back to normal.

"What... what did she say? The 'Daughters will be pleased'?" Mars asked, walking over to help Bastien up to her feet. No one answered her, and she looked back and forth at the two of us, looking for a response.

"What did she mean by that?" she asked again.

"If I had to guess... The Daughters of Dust," Bastien finally replied in between breaths.

"What? Who are they?"

"Hunters... from the Church. For people like us."

"What does that mean, then?"

"How the hell should I know, Mars?" Bastien snapped, pulling her arm away.

"You were going to be one of them, shouldn't you know?"

"Forgive me, I guess I missed orientation. I tried to escape, remember?" They were getting in each other's faces.

"Both of you, shut up!" I yelled, causing them to break away from each other's glares and look at me.

"She's gone, we need to keep moving," I added on, trying to

defuse the situation.

"Quit being naïve, Sid."

"Don't call him naïve when you're the one who won't ever tell us a damn thing, Bastien."

"Leave me alone, it's easy for you to act like you're so morally superior, isn't it?"

"I said shut up!" I yelled once more. "Mars, she's not some oracle we can just claim knowledge from whenever we demand it."

"Yeah—" Bastien started, but I quickly interrupted her.

"And Bastien, we're all trying to grasp at our situation here, you clearly know more than us, and we're all scared. At least try to show an inkling of sympathy."

"So, we just forget about this whole encounter?" she replied with a snarky remark, tying her white hair back once more.

"No! But all we have is each other, we can't let anything get in between us, you know that." They both fell silent as they looked at me, then each other. Finally, with a frustrated growl, they picked up their belongings and made the best attempts we could at wrapping up any cuts or injuries we sustained.

"You know... I was getting my butt kicked before you saved us so... Thank you," Mars finally said, still not making eye contact. I could tell she was still upset.

"Yeah..." Bastien didn't look at her either, and the mood was still tense. We had the sun to follow now, and it looked as if it was already midday. That whole morning, it had seemed nighttime, she must have been that close to us the entire time. That thought was... unnerving. As we started to take our first steps once again, Bastien stopped and turned toward Mars and let out a sigh.

"Sorry."

Chapter 26

It felt as though the seasons had rapidly begun to change as we ventured further north. The wind became ever so slightly chillier, and the flora became less vibrant. We had walked for hours through fields of tall grass and reeds, some even climbing higher to the sky than our heads would reach. The white feathery strands at the crowns of the grass swayed and fluttered wherever the wind took them. They were beautiful, and the soft, moist ground at our feet made the silence of the fields calming. It was a nice reprieve.

We slowly strode and pushed our way through, my hands were becoming raw from pushing so much of the plant life out of the way. Mars, however, had no issues. The reeds and grass seemingly bowed out of her way, making her journey just a leisurely walk.

"You can't have them move out of our way either?" I asked her, still struggling to plan my steps and keep up with her.

"I'm not asking them to." She turned to answer me.

"Well, can you?"

"We're in their home, it's rude to demand they do what you say, don't you think?" I didn't have an answer, and simply rolled my eyes as I kept pushing forward.

"I wonder what this place is going to entail…" Bastien spoke up behind me as she kept my pace. We stopped and both looked back at her.

"You mean, if there will be Sages that had been captured like us?" I asked.

"Yeah, but…" her voice trailed off; something was clearly on her mind.

"Think about it, how can there really be an entire port full of people like us? There can't be that many left…"

"What are you saying?"

"I'm saying, they must have civilians as well. Maybe Sages are just the prized possessions."

"And if Lex is a Sage, maybe there's others working for him as well…" Mars added on, causing Bastien to nod. I didn't want to believe that, that Sages were enslaving our own kind and innocent people as well. I couldn't understand it. It was a naïve thought, I know.

"So, how are we going to protect people while fighting?" Mars asked. Bastien looked at her, then to the ground. It didn't seem either of them had an answer.

"Regardless… we need to destroy that place," I finally spoke up.

"Destroy it…?"

"Yes. Even if we save everyone and it all goes smoothly, what then? Won't they just fill it right back up with others?" I knew I was right, and I knew the others would have no choice but to agree. I was angry. Angry at the thought of us fighting to survive, while our very same kind were seemingly doing everything they could to tarnish our likelihood even more.

"I agree. I want to destroy everything that bastard holds dear." I knew Bastien would agree, she's held onto her resentment toward Lex ever since we escaped Fortuna.

"We need to try and save everyone before we can think about burning that place to the ground."

"We will. But we can't leave anything behind."

"… All right," Mars reluctantly agreed, sighing and turning back to continue on our path. Almost immediately, however, the plants started to thin and grow shorter. I hadn't realized we were already near the edge of this forest of grasses. I stopped to stretch my arms as we took our first steps out into the open once more. The cool breeze blew, sending a chill down my body. We had been protected from the wind while we were trudging our way through, but now were exposed to the elements once more. The sound of waves crashing against the sand and rocks on the beach echoed up toward us. The hill we had found ourselves on gave us a clear view of the lay of the land.

"Did we… head in the right direction?" Mars asked, looking around and saying what we were all quickly noticing; there was no port. There was no evidence of any kind of people being here at all, in fact.

"This is right where we were supposed to go, I'm sure of it."

"What did your cousin say again?" I turned to ask Mars.

"Through the grasses, to the stone. At the feet of the red cliffs."

I looked out once, a rather large boulder was the only thing protruding out of the hill we had found ourselves on. And the cliffs that looked out into the sea were stained red from the Iron bleeding out from the dirt and rock.

"This has to be it, everything matches…" Bastien said, crossing her arms.

"Maybe we're missing something," Mars replied and started to walk back toward the grass forest we had just left. I looked around myself, hoping to see something of relevance or perhaps even a clue. We all looked in silence, pacing back and forth across the hill. My frustration started to grow as I wasn't finding any sort of answer.

My attention was suddenly grabbed by a rather strange, almost mechanical-sounding chirp. I whirled around and was shocked to see a large, black and white bird gliding above. I recognized it from etchings immediately, it was a mage-crow! I had never seen one before, only heard and read about them. Their feathers and plumage changed consistently to match the lunar cycle and were always rumored to only appear to those most in need. Its large wings were spread out as it soared above me. The captivating patterns seemed to glisten on its feathers as its long tail feathers fluttered through the breeze. I watched it in amazement as it started to dive from the sky and pass right into the large boulder nearby. I stood there for a moment, in utter disbelief at what I had just witnessed. I turned to look at the others; they hadn't even noticed the mage-crow like I just had. I always assumed the legends about them meant they only selectively showed themselves, but maybe the others couldn't see it at all.

"Hey! Come here!" I yelled at the other two, grabbing their attention as they hastily came to me.

"This boulder, I think… I don't think it's real."

"What are you talking about?" Bastien asked me, seemingly annoyed.

"I just watched a bird fly into it!" I nearly yelled, pointing toward it. The other two merely looked over the large rock, then back to me. After telling them to watch, I walked up to it and held out my hand, hesitating right before I was about to touch it. I took a deep breath and placed my hand, expecting to just feel the roughness of the stone. But to my surprise, my hand slipped through, causing the rest of the boulder to ripple like I had just placed my hand into a body of water. I could hear the other two run up to me as they saw what had just happened. I pushed my arm further in before taking my first steps through.

I nearly lost my balance at what I had seen; the sky was black and filled with rivers of vibrant pink and violet stars, winding and wrapping around each other in the heavens above. I stood there with my mouth hanging open before Bastien elbowed me in the ribs, pointing to the beach below us. There was an entire shipping dock, and several large yurts strewn across the beach. Of course, this slaver port was hidden. We all stood there in shock, taking in our surroundings. There had to have been at least a dozen slavers down there, and cages that were occupied by people. But worst of all, behind one of the yurts, was a body pit. And it was nearly full.

Chapter 27

I stared in disbelief at what I was seeing. The situation we found ourselves in was more dire than we anticipated. We could see just how big an operation this really was, which would explain why this illusion was needed to cover it. This realm we had found ourselves in seemed to send all of my senses into disarray.

We crouched down behind a rather large bush next to the passageway we had just discovered; its leaves were a bright red with the edges seemingly lined in gold, the colors of everything in the world didn't make any sense. And everything smelled… sweet. It made me uncomfortable seeing how there looked to be dozens of bodies down below us. This had to have been the work of a Sage, a rather powerful one at that if they're able to create an entire dimension that's hidden from the naked eye.

None of us said a word, but I could feel the tension between us. We were all nervous as we were starting to realize more and more how much of an undertaking this would be. I watched as a hastily repaired wooden ship had already set sail away from the docks, slowly becoming more and more transparent as it drifted away from the shoreline; and eventually vanished into thin air. We had already missed one, and who knows how many people were held captive on that ship. We couldn't let another leave. I stood up to try and get a better view of the slavers below us and came to a surprising realization.

"I don't think there's any Sages amongst them," I whispered to the other two as I crouched back down to them.

"Yeah… I was thinking that too. But we still can't be sure. Any one of them could be one… maybe even the one who created this whole place," replied Bastien as she was still observing the port. I felt the hairs on my arms standing up and noticed that my whole body has had chills since we came into this place. Everything here felt… wrong.

"The plants here… I don't think they're real," Mars spoke up, rubbing one of the leaves on the bush in front of us.

"I mean, they are real but… when I reach out, nothing reaches back. It's like they're empty."

"So… does that mean that…?"

"I don't think I'll be able to use my powers in here," Mars replied. The thought of being down a person was worrying.

"Sid, can you still…?" Bastien looked over toward me. I shrugged and looked out toward that body pit that has been capturing my attention since we got here. I slowly reached out my hand toward it, feeling the pull from several of the bodies.

"Yes, but… it's shaky." I attempted to keep control of the tethers I had created, but it seemed like something was causing them to tremble. I dropped my hand and saw one of the arms of the bodies fall back down to its side. I hadn't realized I was pulling that hard on them. One of the slavers near the body pit saw the arm fall, causing him to take several steps back and yell to the others. The three of us quickly jumped down to the ground, worried we had been caught.

We watched as two other slavers made their way over to the panicked guard. I could only hear mumbling between them but saw the one repeatedly point to the body pit. Eventually, the other two approached the bodies with their swords drawn. They must have assumed that there was a survivor. After a quick pointing of their sword to verify that was the one that moved, I could hear a sickening squelch as one of their swords pierced the abdomen. The two slavers waited, then walked back to their posts seemingly unimpressed.

"I can use that against them," I said quietly, still watching the two slavers walk away. My companions looked over at me, puzzled.

"Did you see that? I could raise all of them, cause a panic. The guards would probably leave the captives in order to stop the undead."

"I should be the one to try and open the cages, since I can't do much else in here," Mars added on, already agreeing to my plan and pointing to the stacked and occupied cages that were pushed back against the cliffs on the far side. That would leave me and Bastien to fight off the slavers and protect the captives. It was a daring plan, but more than we had a minute ago.

I stood up and snuck my way down the hill with the other two close behind me. I reached a half-repaired sailboat behind a yurt that was a close distance to the body pit. I could feel a better connection to them now, even if it was still shaky. I only needed them to distract, so it didn't make much of a difference to me as long as we could slip in between the slavers and the cages. After a quick nod to the others, I reached out once more, attaching more and more tethers to the bodies. I felt a strong connection, and I let my power flood through my arms once more. I would need it if I was going to control this many. I just had to keep myself under control, I couldn't afford to lose myself in here, not like last time. With a 'tug' in my mind, I forced them all to slowly clamber over each other and rise out of the pit. Their tattered and blood-stained clothes hanging loosely on their now-clamoring bodies. It took a moment, but the slavers nearby eventually turned around and witnessed the horror in front of them as a dozen had already risen to their feet. It took everything I had to keep my concentration controlling this many, and I felt a bead of sweat trickle down my face. The ringing in my ears muted the panicked yells of the slavers as more and more of them ran over to the pit, eventually leaving the cages unguarded.

"Now, Bastien! Let's go!" Mars grabbed her arm and pulled her away from my side and they ran over to their destination. I had to stay and keep controlling the bodies. They weren't going to be much of a challenge to men with swords, but it could keep them preoccupied, at least for a little bit. I stood up and reached out with both hands in order to have a greater grasp on them, forcing their limp bodies to swing at and lumber over to them. Their swords glistened in the bright starlight above us as a dozen of them started cutting down the bodies. I could feel the tethers snapping as each one was cut down. But I had plenty more to control. I managed to have a couple of them overwhelm one of the guards, smothering him and forcing him to the ground as he yelled. The others quickly started swinging at him in an attempt to cut him loose, but even more started grabbing and biting them from behind. It was a slow endeavor, but I was going to do everything I could to make this a nightmare for them. Anything to give the other two enough time.

I risked a look over, breaking concentration for a moment to see how their progress was going. I witnessed Bastien break a lock with a flash of light and swing one the doors open. Two men and a child slowly came staggering out, their clothes looked ragged, and they looked starved.

"Shit!" I felt several more tethers snap as I let myself get distracted. I whipped my head back to see several of the bodies I had under my grasp fall limp to the ground, the slavers all looking around confused. I blew my cover; I didn't have the time to try and reanimate them. Dammit! I should have given them more time.

I jumped over the sailboat and ran over to Bastien as I watched some of the slavers realize what was going on. I had to fight with her to keep them back and protect Mars while she attempted to pick the locks.

"They're coming!" I yelled, getting their attention. Bastien turned around only to see at least a dozen of them running toward her, swords held high. I had to find some way to help, they had a head start on me already. I stopped in my tracks as I saw Bastien lift her arms above her head, forming at least a hundred small white orbs in the air above her. It looked like snow that had been suspended motionless over her head. She let out a yell and threw her arms down, sending the tiny orbs crashing down into the slavers, each one leaving a trail of light as it flew through the air. Sand and dirt burst into the air as each orb made contact with either a slaver or the ground. It almost looked like several of them had pierced through their bodies as they fell and tumbled, being struck mid-run. It didn't get all of them, but it took out enough of them to give me an opening.

"Hurry! You need to run!" I heard Mars yell as she managed to open another door. A woman walked out from the cage and threw her arms around her savior.

"I know, but you need to go!" I could hear Mars say assuredly to her, almost pushing her away.

I could hear a weak "thank you" from the woman as she turned to make her way toward the hill we had descended down earlier.

She had only gotten a couple of steps in before something whistled past my ear and struck the woman in the stomach, sending her flying back and impaling her against the stone cliff face. It looked like some sort of large spike made out of bone as the starlight reflected off its pale white surface. She weakly grabbed it, struggling in vain as her tunic became more and more saturated with the color red. Quickly, her head dropped, and she let go. She had been killed almost instantly. Me and Mars quickly turned around, shocked at what we had just witnessed.

A man had emerged from one of the far yurts, his skin seemed to be misshapen as if his bones were growing in a very odd way. I watched as something seemed to slither underneath the skin of his arms, only to pierce through the skin of his wrists as he grabbed two more stakes of bone into his hands.

Chapter 28

A bead of sweat ran down my neck as I watched more bones emerge from his wrists. The other slavers stood back, switching their gaze from him to us. I could tell just his presence alone made them feel uneasy. Nobody spoke, I could only hear the heavy breathing from myself and Bastien. I risked a glance over at the slavers we had defeated who were lying still in the sand; I could try to reanimate them in order to fight back. My arms felt weak, I purposely only let a small amount of my power through to keep control of myself, and it was taking a toll. I already felt fatigued. Everything in this… realm felt heavier somehow. Every action was draining. But I couldn't let myself slip up; I don't know what would happen to everyone here if I did.

"I'll be forced to kill you if you continue with this," the Sage finally spoke, his gravelly, hoarse voice breaking the tense silence. I saw him facing Mars. He seemed more preoccupied with the cages than me. I quickly ran over and stood in front of her and gave my best attempt at glaring him down. I had no idea what he could actually do, and it made me nervous, which he apparently noticed as he simply gave out a laugh at my apparent heroic attempt.

"You're a Sage too, how can you allow this to happen?" I shouted, taking a step toward him. His laugh made a wave of anger flood through me. He simply stared back at me, an annoyed look on his face. I waited, but only received a cold glare in return.

"Answer me!"

"Get out of the way!" he shouted back, throwing one of the bone stakes at me. I held my arms over my face to shield myself as I crashed into the sand before me, letting out a loud 'boom' and sending out a shockwave. The impact of it nearly knocked all the breath out of me, and I stumbled back, trying to catch myself. I opened my eyes as a waterfall of the white sand was still falling down all around us. I met his glare once more as he sent his message loud and clear; that was the only warning I'd get. I couldn't believe how strong of a throw he had. If even one of those hit us…

Once more I heard the sickening sound of a stake emerge from his wrists as he grabbed it into his hand. Bastien walked over and stood next to me, her arms outstretched.

"You're not getting past us!" she shouted. The Sage looked even more annoyed, but again did not respond to her. I could hear Bastien let out a frustrated grunt as she stepped toward him. His silence was aggravating her.

"I'm so tired of people like you!" she shouted once more, throwing a bolt of light at him as it whizzed through the air and pierced his shoulder. He didn't even seem to have a reaction to the gaping hole as blood started to seep out of it. Me and her stood there, confused and tense as we waited. He looked over at his new wound, and his skin started to bubble around the edge as it began to close up on its own, eventually sealing it up completely. I gasped as there wasn't any evidence of him being injured, not even a scar.

"What—" Bastien started to speak as a bone stake whistled through the air toward her. He was fast, I could barely react in time. A loud 'crack' rang out as Bastien manifested a shield of light in front of her without a second to spare. Her shield cracked and flickered as it dissipated into sprinkles of light that eventually

171

disappeared. She stumbled a couple of steps back before I grabbed her arm, holding her up on her feet. She hurriedly stood back upright with a gasp and was about to fight back, but a loud cracking noise above caught all of our attention. I looked up, only to see the bone stake that had been deflected had impaled itself into the... sky? Cracks were emerging from every direction around the impact as the stars above us started to fall and hiss into the sand.

"We can destroy this place..." Mars said behind us as she also was looking upward.

"We have a bigger problem right now," I replied, taking one more glance at the bodies that were strewn across the sand. The other slavers had already retreated, leaving us alone with him. After another tense moment of silence, I reached out toward the bodies, straining my body and mind once more as I took hold of one after the other, forcing them to rise to their feet. The Sage raised his arm toward me as if to retaliate, but a blast of light hit him in his arm, distracting him.

"Your fight is with me!" Bastien shouted. She was trying to give me as much time as she could. My gaze kept shooting between the Sage and my growing horde as my head started pounding. I was the familiar black marking start to swirl around my fingers. Good, as long as they kept themselves on my hands, I still had control of myself.

Several more loud 'cracks' rang through my ears as Bastien repeatedly manifested more and more shields to deflect his attacks. I had my opening and commanded the dead I had reanimated to charge and attack him. As they swarmed over toward him, he took notice and reached onto his back. Dozens more cracking and ripping sounds emanated from him as he pulled a huge, spiked mace made out of bone from his back. He swung it wildly at the bodies, obliterating them and sending others flying. I stumbled back as I watched him quickly finish off my creations and make eye contact with me. With a loud grunt he started to run toward me. I crouched down, ready to dive out of the way as he lifted the mace above his head. But before he had a chance to swing, a whip made out of light wrapped around his neck, pulling him back and making him drop his weapon. Me and the Sage looked over to see Bastien behind him, whip in her right hand and a bright, glowing blade covering her left hand. With a loud yell, she lunged toward him.

She was too far away to strike fast enough as he threw a bone stake from his forearm, striking Bastien in the leg and sending her airborne in the opposite direction. She screamed as she slammed and slid in the sand, immediately grabbing her leg as she yelled. The stake pierced clean through her, and she tried to manifest more light in one of her hands, only for it to crackle and sizzle away as he started to walk toward her. I felt panic start to flood through me, I had to do something, or she was going to die.

My mind was blank as I started to run toward him, I had to improvise. But… I felt something, like a tug. I looked over at where I felt it and saw a faint glow coming from the Sage's torso. Was that… his soul?

"Get the hell away from her!" Mars shouted as she jumped in front of her injured comrade. The Sage was distracted, this was my only chance to save them both. I lunged toward him, placing my hand on his back. He started to turn around toward me as I wrapped my hand around the glow and ripped it out. He let out a loud yell that quickly grew silent as I fell to the ground. His body collapsed limp into the sand. I could sense it from him, he was dead. His weapons of bone fell from his hands as he lay there, motionless. I couldn't move as I watched the color of his eyes turn a pale gray. He felt like an empty shell now. I breathed heavily and turned to look back at my shaking hand, the faint glow of his soul shimmered in my palm. But the sphere quickly started to break apart, and I watched in shock as his soul in my hand started to dissipate and become absorbed into me. I felt a surge of strength through me as my body immediately seized up, causing me to roll over onto my stomach, gasping. I felt I had instantly recovered from any fatigue I had previously been experiencing. I felt… reborn. I looked up at Mars, who was already walking over to me. I opened my mouth, but no words came out. Did I just… absorb his soul? She looked at his lifeless body then at me once more, also not saying a word.

With a loud grunt and yell, Bastien threw a small bolt of light into the sky, striking the bone stake that had been impaled into the stars. The cracks grew farther before eventually giving way to a deafening shattering sound. The sky around us burst into dust and the stars all fell back down, sizzling into the sand as they turned into small stones. Daylight came flooding back down as we found ourselves once more within the outside world. Me and Mars looked at each other as we smiled with relief. Her smile quickly faded as she jumped to her feet, looking at the ground around her, then toward Bastien.

"Move! Get out of the way!" She jumped up and ran toward our injured friend, who was still grunting in pain and surrounded by several released captives. I sat up, confused as to what she was going to do. She dropped to her knees and immediately threw her open palms into the sand. After a couple of seconds, I watched as a sprout emerged from the loose ground, quickly growing larger and larger into a huge flower that had bloomed in front of all of us. Mars's hands were shaking as she clenched her teeth, moving her hands along with the flower that was growing in front of our eyes. The black stalk quickly grew wider, and the red and white flower twirled as it fully blossomed.

"This… is going to sting," Mars said in between panting. I jumped to my feet and shakily stumbled over to them as I watched a golden drop of liquid seep from the center of the flower and fall onto Bastien's wound, forcing her to yell through clenched teeth. When I reached them, I saw her wound amazingly slowly close on its own.

"What is that?" I said, pointing at the flower that had performed a miracle in front of my eyes.

"Mystica Rosa… they can heal any wound… but they're almost impossible to come by."

"And one just happened to be here?"

"No, I created it," she said, still trying to catch her breath.

"What do you mean?"

"I can create life as well. But it is… very taxing. I can't do it very often." I looked at the flower once more, still in disbelief at what she had to just done in front of everyone. Bastien even seemed amazed as well as she grabbed her leg, looking it over in disbelief.

"That's… incredible," I replied, still in amazement.

"Not really… it's going to die here. It can't thrive in this environment. I took a life to save a life." I didn't know how to respond to her, instead looking down at Bastien, concerned.

"We can't protect you all anymore, you need to flee," Mars said to the newly freed captives who stood around us.

Only a single woman grabbed her hand, then mine before telling us "Thank you" as she joined the others making their way up the hill we had previously descended.

Chapter 29

"We need to leave before more show up."

The three of us made our way back from where we came. Bastien was still walking with a limp as her leg continued to heal, blood dripping off her soaked trousers and staining the white sand at our feet. Mars told her it should take another day or two for her to feel completely normal again. Her miraculous recovery still left me dumbfounded; I had never known a plant could do that, let alone even hearing of such a remarkable flower. I took one last look behind us down at the beach, the yurts and wooden crates all still standing, left untouched. We had freed everyone, but it still felt like a short lived, hollow victory. How long until they restore this port? Fill those cages again? We had to, somehow, halt this whole operation or else this would never end. We all knew it, even if we didn't say it.

Mars was breathing heavily as she struggled to walk up the hill behind us. I reached out and grabbed her hand, and she wrapped her fingers around my palm. I slowly assisted her the rest of the climb, the hard packed dirt crunching under our feet. They were both fatigued, but I was the one who felt like I had a great night's sleep and full meal. All because I… absorbed that Sage's soul. I was trying to distract myself, but it was proving difficult to forget. The look Mars gave me when she realized what I had done… I never wanted to give her a reason to look at me like that again.

"We should go back to Animas Core… We're too banged up

to defend ourselves," Bastien suggested once we had reached the top of the hill and faced the familiar forest of pampas grass.

"Yeah, I feel like crap right now," Mars replied in a raspy voice, leaning against me for support. Creating that flower really wreaked havoc on her. I simply nodded at them both, trying to keep a stoic expression to hide the worry I had building inside of me over what I had just done. A sudden breeze blew open the dirty and torn tunic I had been wearing, making me shiver. I could barely tell what color it used to be, with all the dirt and sweat stains on it. I turned to take one last look at the carnage we wrought, and nearly gasped. The sun looked to be setting soon as it turned the ocean behind us into a magnificent ray of orange and yellow. I had never seen the ocean before; it was always one of my childhood dreams. It wasn't much of one, and it seemed silly because of how commonplace it was for everyone to have been; but not me. I just wished my dream hadn't been realized like this…

As we neared the grass, I gazed upward as they towered above me. The ends fluttering in the breeze above. Before we could move any further, Mars pulled her hand from me.

"Wait! You're having trouble walking—"

"I'll be okay, trust me." She turned around and cut me off mid-sentence before proceeding to walk into the makeshift trail we created before. Strands of her black hair were dangling in front of her eyes, which showed a downcast expression. She looked tired, not just from the events that had just transpired, but from just trying to survive. She stumbled a couple of times, but the grass surrounding her bent down and held her under her arms, stabilizing her as she went.

"Must be nice," Bastien muttered next to me as she watched Mars, standing with all of her weight on her non-injured leg.

"I could animate a body to help you walk," I replied, holding back a laugh.

"Don't you dare." She quickly shot me a glare, before seeing my smile and realizing I was joking.

"Shut up," she added on as she pushed me aside, walking after Mars. I let out a laugh as I fell in tow behind them both. The towering reeds kept swaying in the wind, blocking out what little sunlight we had left. The ground was getting difficult to see as my eyes were struggling to adjust to twilight. The dead or broken twigs snapped under our feet, and I absent mindedly turned it into a game, trying to find the largest and loudest I could step on and break. After a while of silent trail blazing, we found ourselves at the battleground from the other day, where the so-called 'Daughter of Dust' attacked us. The small craters blasted into the dirt where she had landed at each of us were still prevalent, laying undisturbed.

"We're almost back to our last campsite, should we stay there again?" I asked.

"Yeah…" Bastien was looking down at the ground around us, still visibly upset at what had transpired here. I wanted to ask her how she ended up almost becoming one of them, but it was probably best saved for another time. Before long we had arrived at our destination, the charred remains of the wood from our campfire were still there, just as we left it. I had helped them lay out their bedrolls, and almost immediately I could hear light snoring from both of them and they nearly collapsed onto them. Their exhaustion quickly overtook the two. Before long, I joined them in a deep slumber as well.

*

I shot awake, gasping. I struggled to get my eyes to adjust as I rubbed them. It was so dark, there were no stars. My stomach dropped as I let my arms fall back to my side and I heard a splashing noise. I sat up, and my breathing became shaky as I realized I was back in the abyss… again.

My legs seemed to wobble before I steadied myself upon standing. The splashes of the black liquid echoed throughout as I slowly walked blindly forward.

"Open the halls…" That voice rasped again in the darkness. I stopped in my tracks. It spoke to me immediately. It felt as if… it had been expecting me. I felt afraid, but also angry.

"What does that mean?" I yelled back, waiting anxiously. I kept spinning around, waiting for that hand to appear once more. I was going to be ready this time, I was not going to let it near me.

"The prophecy of blood and soul must be realized." It boomed once more, making me jump. It was coming from every direction and sounded to be made of dozens of voices all speaking in unison. I breathed deeply, trying to build up my courage to respond.

"I don't know what you're saying!" I yelled back into the darkness. Again, silence. I could only hear my heavy breathing and my heart pounding in my ears. My adrenaline was going into overdrive, and I felt light-headed.

"What prophecy?" I asked in a quieter tone of voice as I quickly realized I was probably not going to get any answers. Almost immediately I heard a loud boom behind me as I whirled around, only to see a massive black wave rushing toward me. I threw my arms up to shield myself from the crashing liquid, but it split and rushed around me before reforming behind me. I dropped my arms in surprise as I watched the walls of the rushing

179

black water roar past me before finally subsiding to its calm state as before.

Off in the distance from where it originated from was a faint, red glow. I took one more cautious look behind me as I slowly made my way toward the dim light. I started breathing heavier as the cold air made my throat and nostrils burn. Once I got close enough and was able to see what I couldn't make out in distance, I gasped. It was the same hand that had grabbed me before, emerging from the liquid at my feet. The countless children's hands that created its form were wiggling and moving around seemingly on their own. However, it was motionless, and holding... a dagger? I took another cautious step closer trying to inspect it more. The curved blade was rusted, with unfamiliar runes etched into it. The handle seemed to be made of a sort of black wood, which had a strange marking carved into it as well. The hand let go and slid back down into the liquid, the rumble at my feet made me jump back.

"Awaken your power..." the voice said once more, trailing off into a whisper as it fully descended out of sight, leaving only ripples. The dagger floated motionless in place. I hesitated and looked around me once more. I didn't seem to have much of a choice, and I could feel it... calling me. I don't know why, but I had to take it. It felt like an impulse. Slowly, I reached out and wrapped my hand around the wooden handle.

I shot up, gasping as I realized I was back at the campsite once more. The other two shot up as well, staring at me confused. My gasp must have been loud enough to awaken them. I could feel the cold sweat running down my face as I tried to catch my breath. It felt as if I hadn't been breathing that whole time.

"What's wrong? Are you all right?" Mars asked me, rubbing her eyes.

"Yeah, sorry… just a nightmare," I replied. I wanted to tell them the truth but… what could I even say? I didn't know myself.

"Well… try to get some sleep. We have quite a hike ahead of us tomorrow." She laid back down onto her bedroll and turned over to her other side. I didn't respond and simply nodded, finally getting my breathing under control. I attempted to wipe the sweat from my forehead, but my similarly sweaty hand only made it worse.

"What is that?" Bastien asked me. I saw her looking down at my other hand. I looked back down myself, confused at what she was asking. My eyes bulged once I saw what she was talking about; the rusted dagger from my dream, it was laying there in the same grip I had grasped it with.

Chapter 30

My hand trembled as we were both staring at the haunting object in my palm. The moonlight reflecting off the sharpened edge, the only part of it not stained with rust. I looked up at Bastien, who in turn looked up and made eye contact.

"I grabbed it... off a slaver as a while ago," I panicked, saying the first thing that came to mind. I sat there, tense as I watched her give me a puzzled look, then down at the dagger once more. For blurting out a made-up reason as to why I had this now, I suppose it could have been worse.

"What is that carved all over it?" I shrugged at her question, forcing myself to keep my mouth shut.

"Well, we should probably get going since we're all awake anyways." She brushed it off, seemingly accepting my answer. I felt awful lying, but I couldn't give her a real answer as to where it came from. I didn't even know myself. She gave a gentle kick to Mars's leg, and she groaned and sat up as we started to pack up our belongings. I kicked some dirt into the charcoal of our fire the night before, hoping to cover up any evidence of people staying here. I was still nervous of being followed because of that woman that attacked us. I adjusted my tunic, brushed my hair out of my face, and carefully slid the blade into my belt loop. I watched the sky start to glow a pale orange and pink, signaling the sun starting to rise over the horizon. I stared in a trance, waiting for the warmth of the light to hit me. It offered a nice distraction from my thought for the time being, but quickly faded as my mind brought me back to my dream once more.

The other two kept pace almost in tandem in front of me. I caught myself staring down at my feet, zoning in and out. Why did I keep having these… dreams? Where was that dark place I kept finding myself in? And that black liquid, it felt more viscous than water, and for some reason it seemed to avoid causing me any harm. All of these questions didn't unnerve me as much as that voice, that being that seems to reside there. I would've just chalked this up as a recurring nightmare if it wasn't for the bruise I had on my arm and now this dagger. It clearly wants me to do something, or wants something from me, but what? Every time I seem to grow my powers, I find myself in that place once I fall asleep. Maybe the only way to find answers is to keep going. Still, I couldn't shake the uneasy feeling of the words it spoke to me last night. What prophecy was it speaking of? And what-

"Sid," I snapped out of my trance to see Mars looking back at me.

"We're coming up on Animas Core." I looked past her to see the outlines of buildings in the distance. Already? How long was I zoning out for? It must have been hours. These dreams must really be impacting me, I felt mentally exhausted… MY feet suddenly started aching as I came back to reality, and the fatigue quickly spread throughout my legs. I really had been walking mindlessly for a long time.

As we neared the outskirts, we all pulled our hoods over our heads once more and cautiously made our way through the dirt streets. The small pebbles in the trail through town rattled under our feet, and I saw the runoff stream from the mine still flowing unopposed through one of the walkways. After doing our best to avoid the residents, we finally arrived at Ezre's home. Otto sat perched in the front window and gave an excited meow when he saw us approaching. Mars darted past Bastien and pushed the front door open, scooping up her gray and white cat into her arms.

"My handsome young man!" she said happily as she kissed him repeatedly.

The wooden floorboards creaked as I made my way inside, pulling my hood down and closing the door behind us. Ezre came out from one of the back rooms, still cleaning the soot off himself from another day of work.

"Oh! It's great to see you all back. What happened out there?" he said, surprised. The three of us gave each other a serious look.

"We... saved some people, and quickly left and came back," Mars spoke up before we could, leaving out a lot of details. I didn't try to correct her, I could understand the thought of the less he knows, the better.

"Oh. Well, please make yourselves at home. I haven't had the chance to clean up, so you'll have to forgive me." He simply nodded at the lack of information, seemingly in agreement that he didn't want to know too much either. After we quickly set our belongings down in one of the back rooms, Mars pulled me aside as Ezre continuously asked Bastien about the capital city of Artessa.

"I'm going to go into the forest, do you want to come with me? I'm assuming you need to decompress too," she asked me. I smiled at her and nodded. We quickly darted past the two, who were too engrossed in their discussion to notice.

The jaunt into the tree line on the edge of town was peaceful. The fir trees stood valiantly as we did our best to duck and slip past the extending branches. There was no wind, the birds were singing, I felt relaxed for the first time in a long time. We quickly found ourselves at a clearing, revealing a fairy ring on the ground; a large group of mushrooms in a circle emerging from the grass.

"Our actions won't go unnoticed, you know that, right?" Mars looked up at me as she crouched down to inspect the flora surrounding us.

"Yeah…" my voice trailed off as I looked away. I knew she was right, but I didn't want to admit it. I had just been pushing it to the back of my mind, I found it had been more comforting than facing that reality.

"I'm not giving up, and you had better not either." She took my hand, making our eyes meet. Her amber eyes glistened in the sunlight cascading over the nearby tree canopy.

"Never." I squeezed her hand as she pulled away, turning to walk into the center of the fairy ring. She looked picturesque as she let her long black hair down, letting it fall down over her shoulders like a crashing waterfall.

"You know, ever since I met you, it seems like we're always fighting for our survival," she said to me, once more turning to face me.

"I'm sorry. I'm trying to become strong—"

"Stop. You didn't let me finish," she spoke up, cutting me off mid-sentence. I felt ashamed of what she said, and I felt somewhat responsible for it all, for some reason.

"It's true, we always seem to be fighting for our survival since I met you. But I've never felt more alive." Her words made me nearly gasp. I blinked at her a couple of times, my mouth hanging open. I was caught so off guard I didn't know what to say.

"You… really?" I managed to stutter out a response, the confusion clearly showing on my face.

"Of course!" She smiled at me. And I smiled back at her. I

quickly realized I could never resist doing so when it came to her.

"It's weird to admit, but I've never been happier," I replied. It felt like a boulder was lifted off my shoulders, like I finally found the true meaning of my feelings. She grinned back at me, and we shared a moment of silence gazing into each other's eyes.

"I need to meditate here, but I'm afraid I will have to be alone," she said in a regretful tone of voice.

"Oh. Yeah, of course." I slowly turned back toward the way we came. I didn't want to leave, but I wasn't going to tell her no.

"Be careful," she said as he waved me goodbye.

"How will you know if I made it back okay?" I replied jokingly.

"The plants will tell me. And they'll never let anything happen to you. Not as long as I'm here." She smiled at me once more as I turned to head back through the forest. Everything seemed to be in chaos in the world around me, but none of it mattered now. Of everyone I could have run into in my biggest time of need, it was her. What an odd twist of fate.

Chapter 31

Night fell, and Mars still hadn't returned from the forest. Bastien, Ezre and I had a lively conversation to make the hours pass by. We talked about our upbringings, our ambitious hopes for the future. Some were subtle, others grandiose. I wanted to live in a place where there were no societal molds, no societal expectations, where variances to our everyday lives were welcomed, not feared. I'm sure I seemed idealistic to the others, but it felt good to be able open up like that regardless.

Eventually, and mercifully, Mars swung the front door open. She looked exhausted and was covered in dirt. We watched her make her way to the back room as Ezre asked if she would like some of the food we prepared, getting only a dismissing wave and a shake of her head. And just like that, she was on her bedroll going to sleep. The three of us quickly decided we probably should as well, as it was getting rather late.

I tossed and turned as I tried to get comfortable but was having no luck of the sort. I didn't even feel tired, and the attempts to force myself asleep were proving unsuccessful. I sat up, frustrated. I rubbed my eyes and made eye contact with Otto, who was curled up on top of Mars's feet.

"You couldn't sleep either?" I heard Bastien ask from across the room. She was sitting up too, leaning against the wooden wall with her arms crossed. I shook my head.

"All right, come on." She beckoned me as she stood up.

"Where are you going?" I asked in a hushed tone.

"To get some fresh air. And you're coming with," I stared at her confused for a moment, but just shrugged and stood up as I didn't have a good reason to refuse. Upon following her carefully toward the front door, we watched our steps so as to not make too much noise. Once we crept outside, she made her way around the side of the house and started climbing up the wooden ladder on leaning against the wall, beckoning me to follow.

"The roof?" I asked from the bottom.

"Quit being a killjoy and come on." She looked back down to say to me. I gave one last look around us to make sure no one was watching and grabbed onto the rungs in front of me. The ladder groaned under my weight as I followed her up to the top. The weather and sun clearly took its toll on it over the years, and I took care as to where I placed my hands in fear of getting splinters. As we reached the slanted, wooden roof, I saw Bastien already sitting on the edge, her feet hanging over the side. I sat next to her, and we both watched in silence at the full moon shimmering its light down onto us. It was a serene night, with no clouds and fields of stars as far as the eye could see.

"I wonder how Sparrow is doing," she spoke up, still looking up at the lunar body.

"If anyone is causing her trouble, I'd feel sorry for them right about now."

"It's still funny to me how shocked we all were back in Fortuna. That little girl turning into… a damn near Demi-god," Bastien replied, chuckling to herself. I laughed back. It was still hard to believe. I knew though, that wherever she was, she was going to be just fine. She seemed resourceful like that.

"So… what are you going to do? After everything, I mean. You never really said earlier." I turned to look at her, and she was already shaking her head.

"You really had to bring up a heavy question like that?"

"Why not? I hardly know anything about you." I leaned back, bracing my arms behind me to hold myself up. I honestly didn't expect much of a reply, maybe even a sarcastic remark. Instead, however, we sat there in silence once more as we both looked out on the horizon.

"… I guess I have been rather closed off, haven't I?" she finally muttered, just loud enough for me to hear. I sat back up, looking at her expectantly.

"I don't know what I'm going to do. I can't exactly go back home… I guess I'll have to wing it."

"You can't go back home? Because of your father?" I asked. She simply nodded, still not looking at me.

"Because you're a Sage?"

"No. It's more than that." She quipped back. I blinked a couple of times, waiting for her to continue. After a moment, she looked over at me before turning back away and sighing.

"Remember when I told you that my father… was convinced I was going to be born a boy. Even went so far as to say, 'God told him so.' He chose the name 'Bastien' months before I was even supposed to arrive. Didn't you ever wonder why a girl would be named that?" I looked away and down at my feet, thinking for a moment.

"It's like Mars said before, I've only heard of men being named that."

"Exactly. So, I'm sure you can imagine the disappointment when I was born." She curled her hands into fists. She was clearly still bitter about all of it.

"And you said he stormed out, right?"

"Yes. He wasn't even a part of my life growing up. My mother raised me alone. She… was the only one at the time who loved me regardless. My life was fine, too. I may have not been what my father wanted but being the child of a Craven still afforded us some luxuries in the capital."

I looked over at her once more. I wanted to be sympathetic, but knowing her, that would just make her angry.

"So then… how did your father come into all of this?"

"Because of my powers… I must have been six or seven when I started showing signs. I would accidentally break something here and there when it would come bursting out of me. Then he suddenly took an interest in me. I went from only seeing him every other holiday to every weekend. I was thrilled about it, but I was too naive to know he just wanted to use me." She took one more deep sigh before pausing.

"And then when everyone started to realize that my powers centered around light, like Viscount Alfonso all those years ago. Except, I obviously could manifest it into physical forms, so it was a little different. But he didn't care, he was obviously ecstatic." The more she revealed about herself, the more I started to understand as to why she resented him.

"He wanted to train me. Of course, I agreed. I couldn't have guessed at the time he just wanted to advance his career and status."

"What about your mother? Did she want this for you, too?"

"No. She protested him every step of the way. Practically begging him to not expose me. Eventually, he grew tired of her and… before I knew it, I was only living with him. I don't know what happened to her, or where she went. Weirdly enough though, my father and I were getting along really well as I grew up. I actually enjoyed the training he put me through." She stopped once again and looked down at her feet. I thought I saw her lip tremble for a moment. She must have missed what she had with him.

"You don't have to continue, if it's too hard."

"I'm fine, Sid. Quit treating me like I'm a child," she snapped, shooting me a glare.

"Okay, sorry. What happened between you two, then?" I asked, quickly changing tone. She looked at me in the eyes for an uncomfortably long time before looking away.

"He… caught me… with my girlfriend." I leaned forward to force her to make eye contact with me again.

"Why would that be an issue?" I asked her.

"What?" She sat back up, giving me a confused look. I didn't respond, giving a confused look of my own.

"You don't care?" she asked, looking visibly annoyed now.

"No. Why would I?"

"It's just—" She stopped herself mid-sentence and turned away from me, seemingly stopping herself from saying something.

"Everyone that knew always reacted with shock or disgust," she finally said in a calm tone. It wasn't her revelation that caught me off guard just now, but her willingness to be this vulnerable. I hadn't seen any of the sort from her before.

"But… that was the last straw for my father. He had me sent to a holding cell almost immediately. He told me I was wrong, and that I needed to repent my ways and accept God once more."

"And what did you do?"

"I refused. Vehemently. But in that cell was when I learned that my powers flourished under strong emotions. I was so angry and afraid that it just… exploded out of me. I blasted my cell door open, injuring the soldier standing guard over me…" I could see her anger and resilience that I had known her for start to return.

"And that… was when I was sent to be conscripted into the

Daughters of Dust. The affirmative gesture that proved that I had been given up on. And… well… you already know what happened when I tried to escape from that place. Your crush ended up saving me, and here we are." I blushed and I turned away immediately, embarrassed. I thought I was being sly about how I felt. She looked over and saw me turning away and laughed.

"Oh, come on, did you really think I didn't notice? You wear your heart on your sleeve." I gave an embarrassed chuckle in return before rubbing the back of my neck.

"But anyways… I can't say I blame you if you look at me differently now. Everyone usually does." I shook my head and looked back up at the full moon with her once more.

"You're the still the Bastien I've known. I actually envy you, in fact." She looked over at me but stayed silent.

"You're so… Valiantly you. Nothing is going to make you someone you're not, and you refuse to pretend. I envy that about you." She stared at me surprised for at least a minute before slowly looking back down at the ground beneath us.

"I… I'm not used to being complemented," she said quietly, clearly feeling awkward. I grabbed a corner of the bread I had brought up with me, tearing it off and flinging it at her, laughing. She looked back up at me as it bounced off her shoulder, giving a laugh in return. Anything to lighten the mood.

We spent several more moments talking about random things in the world and our thoughts on them, but an orange, flickering glow from behind us caught my attention. I turned and looked over my shoulder to see a butterfly with wings made out of flames fluttering down toward me from the night sky above. Bastien was looking up confused at it as well. It slowly made its way down in front of me and fluttered in place. The heat emanating from its wings was making my skin tingle. I reluctantly held out an open palm and the wings extinguished themselves with a subtle hiss, its body falling into my hand. I gave Bastien a confused look and then realized I was holding a small rolled up piece of parchment, the butterfly appeared to have been a message. Giving one more look at my companion I slowly unrolled the parchment, its singed edges crumbling away. My eyes grew wide as the neatly written letters appeared before me. "Come and realize your true destiny, 'Saviors,' where we had our fated first meeting."

Chapter 32

The singed piece of parchment laid ominously in my hand, the words staring at me as if taunting me, waiting for a reaction. I looked up at Bastien who was giving me a puzzled look.

"What does it say?" she asked, as I reluctantly handed it over to her. She cautiously pinched the edge and took it from my hand. I watched her become more and more angry as she read it, before rolling it back up and stuffing it in her pocket. I stared at her until she finally looked up at me.

"We're never going to be rid of our problems, are we?" I asked her, feeling defeated.

"Not unless we rid the world of them ourselves," she replied in a stoic voice. I didn't respond, but instead shook my head and looked down at my feet which were still hanging over the edge. The torn up and dirty shoes were a reminder of how I came from nothing; that in the eyes of this world, I was nothing. My kind have been viewed as cretins, only to be feared and hated.

"Yeah, let's do it," I finally responded, anger building in myself as well.

"Well, that was easy to convince you."

"I'm tired of running away. I'm going to change this world whether it wants to or not. I'm not going to hold back any more." I shot her a look of fiery determination. To my surprise, a grin slowly grew across her face before she jumped to her feet. I slowly stood up as well, all the while giving her a confused look. Before I could say anything, she grabbed me and pulled me in to squeeze me in a hug. I froze, stunned.

"Thank you," she said, muffled against my tunic.

"What?"

"For understanding me." I blinked a couple of times as the realization started to come to me. All her rage and defiance, I now saw why. I wrapped my arms around her as well, hugging her tightly.

"Everything is going to change because of us," I said quietly to her. She pulled away and held a fist up.

"We're done running." She mimicked my own words. I smiled and nodded, then met my fist with hers.

"I swear if you ever tell anyone I hugged you…" she said, threatening me as we started to make our way down the ladder off the rooftop.

"I wouldn't dare," I replied in a joking tone, but I very well knew that she just might actually kill me if I told anyone. We seemed to have been up on top of the house for a while, and the drowsiness was finally starting to set in. We snuck our way back inside, taking care not to make too much noise on the creaking floorboards and wake anyone. When we both arrived at the back room, Mars was still sound asleep as we were greeted by an inquisitive meow from Otto, who was also still in his same position as when we left.

"We'll tell her in the morning, we need to rest first." I turned and whispered to Bastien, who only gave me a nod before we collapsed onto our bedrolls. Mercifully, sleep overtook me almost immediately.

Daylight flooded in the window above me, making me groan as I opened my eyes to see the blurry outline of Mars and Bastien talking amongst each other. I blinked and rubbed my eyes, I didn't know how much sleep I had gotten, but it didn't feel like enough.

"Good, you're awake," Bastien said to me, noticing me stirring. I gave a slow nod as I forced myself to sit up and face them.

"I already told Mars what happened last night." I looked between the two of them, surprised.

"It has to be Lex… right?" Mars asked us both.

"The fire, the theatrics, and summoning us back to Fortuna? I'm positive it's him," Bastien replied. We all sat there in silence for a minute, seemingly deep in thought.

"We need to end this… Are you coming with us?" I asked Mars, who immediately shot me a look as if I had just insulted her.

"You really think you have to ask me that?" she quipped back. I shrugged at her, unsure how to respond.

"Obviously, I'm coming. Since when have I shied away from fighting for what's right?"

I responded with a smile, confirming I knew that she was right.

"But, before we go, I need to prepare," Mars added on as she hesitantly stood up and stretched, before reaching down and picking up Otto so he could climb onto her shoulder.

"Don't wait up, we'll be gone a while." And just like that, she fastened her pack over her shoulder, pulled her hood over her head, and they headed out the front door and out of sight.

"Where is she going?" I turned to ask Bastien.

"I don't know. She can handle herself," she replied, shrugging. We both stood up and made our way out into the main room of the house. I didn't see Ezre anywhere, he must have already headed out for the day. I pulled out one of the wooden chairs, creaking as it slid across the wooden floor.

"Back when we were in those cells... You knew Lex from before, didn't you?" I asked Bastien as she also pulled a chair out to sit down.

"Yeah... well, not personally. The Church, my father mostly, had dealings with him in the past. I had always just assumed he was a mercenary or something of the like. Everyone seemed scared of him. I'd overhear rumors of just how strong he is." I stared at her for a moment before looking down at the table in front of me.

"And now we've made enemies with him."

"Lucky us..." she replied, before taking a bite of the bread that had laid on a dish in the center of the table.

The day quickly flew by as I did my best to try and mentally prepare myself for what lay ahead. I was almost positive I would have to unleash my full potential once more, but I'd have to do everything I could to remain in control. I clearly had no idea what to expect, and soon my mind was awash with different scenarios playing out in my mind of the looming confrontation.

As twilight had started to show itself, Mars returned from her excursion, slowly stepping into the house through the front door. She was covered in dirt and leaves, which she weakly picked off herself and dropped to the floor. Otto himself looked rather tired as well as he slowly rose up to his feet, struggling to keep his balance on her shoulder.

"Where were you?" I asked, observing her as my confusion grew.

"Let's just go to sleep," she replied in a tired tone. I couldn't argue with that, I had a headache all day from the lack of sleep, and I'm sure Bastien was the same way.

The three of us made our way to the back room once more. Mars did her best to pat all the dirt and dust off her before she collapsed in the bedroll with her cat in her arms. Me and Bastien both reluctantly lay down as well without saying a word. We were all of a like mind on what we had to do tomorrow, but the tension was still immense. No one said it, but the nerves were taking hold.

The next morning, we all quickly packed our belongings. After reaffirming with each other, the three of us said our goodbyes to Ezre and headed out in the early morning. We scurried through the gravel streets, trying to keep to the receding shadows as the morning sun started to show itself. We waited a moment behind a stone wall in disarray, and bolted the first chance we got, once again avoiding any inquisitive pedestrians. Only when we reached the entrance to the Canyon of Chains did we stop and take a moment to collect ourselves as we all stared into the familiar trail we once traversed.

"What did you dream about last night?" Mars asked me, still looking forward toward our path. I looked over at her as if seeking clarification as to why she would ask me that, but the only answer I got was her meeting my gaze. She looked... scared. I scrunched my eyebrows, trying to remember the details.

"I don't remember much but... we were side by side. There wasn't any pain or hate... we were free." She looked away to face forward once more.

"That sounds... nice."

Chapter 33

The cool morning breeze blew through the canyon, sending shimmering sand striking against our ankles. The clouds rolling overhead passed over the sun one at a time, offering a brief respite from the solar rays coming down upon us. We walked in tandem and in silence, the gravity of our mission we set ourselves on weighed heavily on each of us, and we were each left to our own thoughts as we progressed forward. I felt exhausted, and I just wanted to stop and rest, but I knew we couldn't, not with a threat like this looming over our heads.

I kept hearing the faintest noise, what sounded like a whisper. I couldn't make out what it was saying, but it was clearly a voice. It sounded... fleeting, like a wisp in the wind. I looked back behind me, only to see the rock walls of the canyon and footprints in the sand. There was no one behind us. The other two gave no reaction either as they continued to keep pace in front of me.

Silence returned once more as I did my best to shake off the voices I was hearing and pressed on behind Mars. My mind wandered to the all-too-familiar question of *why me?* I found myself asking that more and more frequently as of late. Why was I the one that had to become a Sage? And not only that, but these powers that I had? Me and everyone I had known growing up were taught that Sages could have a vast array of powers, but none could control the very fabric of life itself. That is, until I came along. It was easy to start believing in some 'divine plan' when you have cast doubt upon yourself. I nearly slipped into that mindset myself, wanting to believe there was a reason for my existence, and a reason for the events that had transpired to me. Maybe that's why so many people follow the teachings of the Church so devoutly, it offers a comforting answer to an otherwise unpleasant question. An easy escape for those not brave enough to face the unknown or embrace change. I couldn't exactly blame them; my escape, powers, even dreams were frightening to me. In all honesty, sometimes, I just wanted to run from it all, to hide. Moments of weakness. I always shook the thought from my head. It wasn't an option, not anymore.

"The easy way out is for the weak." I remembered my sister, Allison, saying those words to me when I was younger. I was being bullied by some other boys in my town and ran crying to her. I wanted to just hide from them, and she reprimanded me for it. They were harsh words, but I saw now there was at least a crumb of truth to them.

The faint whispers returned once more and I spun around, ready to see who was behind us. Again, nothing. But I could still hear them, and it sounded like multiple people this time, all speaking in unison. Except I realized the sound wasn't coming from behind but from… I dagger? I looked down to my thigh at the rusted blade tied to my leg with two bits of twine. It almost seemed to be… vibrating as I looked directly at it, and the voices grew louder.

"I remember this spot." I heard Bastien say ahead of me, making me snap out of my trance and look over at where the other two were. The voices stopped immediately as I looked away. She was pointing at a lone juniper tree jutting out from behind a rather large boulder.

"This was where we stopped running, and Sparrow found us,

right?" Mars added on. I quickly walked up to them as Bastien nodded at Mars.

"Which means... we've still got a long way to go," Mars added on with a sigh.

The daytime grew hotter and hotter as the sun quickly rose directly overhead. We all had our hoods pulled over our heads to try and shield our faces. A couple more hours passed, and the desert landscape of the canyon all started to blend together. My calves started to burn after walking for so long through this soft sand. How did we run so far when we escaped Fortuna?

Eventually, the three of us stopped when we reached a dead tree that was protruding from the canyon wall, its large branches hanging over the path ahead. My stomach turned as I saw what was in front of us. A body, hanging by a noose from one of the branches. A sack was thrown over their head, and torn, ragged clothes were barely holding together upon a clearly emaciated corpse. Around the neck, however, was a wooden sign that was draped down over the chest by a bit of rope that read, "Consequence." In crude writing. We all looked at it in silence for a moment, and the sick feeling I originally felt turned to anger.

"Lex. It had to have been. Trying to say this was our fault," I spoke up, my anger placing a growl in my voice.

"Another one of his slaves, snuffed out needlessly," Mars replied.

"Come on, we're not going to let him get to us with this." Bastien strode past the body, beckoning toward us to follow. She was right, Lex was trying to play mind games with us. It's not like we could do anything for that person now. It had already seemed like we had been walking all day, and the sun setting behind us all but confirmed it. Thankfully, the canyon was starting to widen, indicating we were reaching the end.

"We should stop here for the night. Going into Fortuna tired would only get us killed." I grabbed Bastien's shoulder, and she quickly agreed. We could see the desert town in the distance, its haunting image seemed to taunt us as it stood proudly in the dry climate. I found a large enough rock to sit down on, mercifully getting off of my feet. We rolled out our now well-used bed rolls as the sky quickly started to darken overhead. Mars and Bastien struck up a conversation as my attention once more returned to the mysterious dagger on my thigh.

"You didn't get that off a slaver, did you?" I looked up, alarmed to see Bastien squinting at me, along with Mars.

"I... No." I wanted to just lie and deflect the topic, but I had to come clean at some point. They stared at me expectantly.

"This isn't going to make any sense but... it came to me, from a dream." The other two continued to stare as their expressions turned from inquisitive to downright confusion. I shared a look back at both of them and took a deep sigh.

"I keep having these... dreams. It seems like every time I do something significant with my power, that next time I fall asleep I find myself in some dark abyss... The first time was in the Golden Forest, right after I ran into you two."

"A recurring dream where it's just darkness?" Mars asked.

"Not just that, but there's something there with me. I don't know who, or what, it is. The first time I was there, I fell through this dark ocean at my feet. Like I said, it was after I ran from home, when I first met you two. Then after we escaped Fortuna... It spoke to me in another dream, at Ezre's house. And it grabbed my arm. I awoke with a bruise on my arm and tried to shake it off. But then it happened again after we left that shipping port. It spoke to me again and handed me... this. I awoke with it in my hand." I pulled the dagger from its makeshift sling and held it up so they could see it.

"Back in the canyon, I could've sworn it was whispering to me." The other two leaned in to inspect the rusted blade in my hand, then looked up at me with the same shocked expression.

"That... thing in your dreams, what does it say to you?" Bastien asked.

"'Open the halls...' and 'the prophecy of blood and soul must be realized.'"

"The timing of all of this seems... convenient, doesn't it? You must have that dagger for a reason," Bastien replied, crossing her arms.

"Sure, but how do we know it isn't with malicious intentions?" Mars turned to ask her.

"We don't. I just know that it's tied to my powers... somehow," I quickly replied.

"Well, today sure got... ominous," Bastien added on, taking one more look at me.

"I'm sorry I didn't say anything sooner, I—"

"Stop. That's a lot to process, I'm glad you trusted us enough to tell us." Mars held up her hand to stop me from talking. I could only give a nod back to her.

"Not to try and change topics but, we need to try and get some sleep before tomorrow," I finally said after clearing my throat and sheathing the dagger on my thigh once more. The other two agreed and we settled in for what I was sure would be a restless night. I lay there staring up at the night sky for what felt like an eternity. There must have been clouds, because there were no stars that could be seen. It wasn't fair, if this was going to go badly, I wanted to at least see the stars one more time.

"Do you... think we'll win?" I asked, breaking the silence.

The worry lay heavily on my mind, and I wasn't sure what kind of answer I was expecting. I just wanted to know I wasn't the only one who was afraid.

"Honestly... I'm unsure we'll survive," Mars replied in hushed tone after a tense moment of silence.

"We have one advantage over him..." Bastien spoke up, and I turned to look in her direction in the darkness.

"He has everything to lose. But us... we're Sages. We were already born in the grave."

Chapter 34

Birds sang vividly all around us as the morning sun started to peek over the horizon. I reluctantly opened my eyes and took in the red and orange glow of the clouds above. The world seemed to weigh heavily down on me ever more so the longer I lay awake.

"I suppose it's now or never," I forced myself to say as I sat up to face the others. They were both silent and gave slow nods in return. We were all nervous. No, we were scared. Mars gave Otto a long kiss on his head that made him scrunch up in disagreement before she finally let go. The somber mood lay over us like a weighted blanket, making the air seem heavier than usual. We didn't say a word as we packed up our belongings once more and took one long look at the outlines of Fortuna in the morning mist.

"I still don't like this," Bastien mumbled after a minute or two of hesitation from all of us.

"If not us, then who?" Mars replied, shooting her a look of determination. It surprised me especially; had her nerves already gone? Or was she just masking it well?

"What would happen to my family if I cowered away? Or even Otto?" she added on, exchanging looks between us.

"I don't have a family like you do—"

"You have us. And we have you," Mars interrupted Bastien mid-sentence, causing her to look over, surprised. I could feel the anger in Mars's voice, her disdain toward those who wished others harm was evident.

I took a deep sigh, and with a heavy foot, I reluctantly took the first step with the other two following suit. I forced myself to press on, fighting every instinct I had to turn around. A million thoughts were running through my mind, different scenarios and how they would play out, trying to guess at what to expect. But the most prevalent one that kept appearing was that this might be my last day alive. I could see in the distance the same cliffside we had descended from before, the Golden Forest standing gracefully upon the plateau. It was disheartening, really. I wanted to appreciate the beauty of this world and all it had to offer, especially with some of the incredible landscapes we had found ourselves in. Maybe if we somehow managed to survive this, I could go. It sounded peaceful, just the thought of even having a future with no strife or worry. I suppose that really is what we were all fighting for in the end.

After what seemed like the longest walk of my life, we reached the town standing defiantly in the desert. I slowly crept up to the brown wall of the nearest building and peeked around the corner. The alleyway was empty and looked as if no one had traversed it in some time. Perfect, maybe we could sneak our way through here. I beckoned for the others to follow as I carefully made my way through, taking care to duck under windows and dart past doorways, several of which caught my eye. Bright colors were painted as decorations around doorways and window frames, much of which was now faded. One, however, had lines of the chorus scribbled around the edges, only to be crossed out with black paint. A clear sign of rebellion against the Church's most common sermon.

I forced myself to break free from my observation of my surroundings and continued down our path. It was going shockingly well. As I reached the corner at the end, however, I realized that we had come upon the plaza. I pressed my back against the cracked wall and took a deep breath before risking a peek. I was expecting to see the same bustling town as before, but to my shock, there was… no one. Not a soul in sight. The wind blew ominously, kicking up sand that had grown loose from the lack of foot traffic. I stood up and walked around the corner to face the silence head-on. The other two also came up beside me, scanning our surroundings in confusion. Bastien was the first to step forward into the suddenly abandoned town. She stopped at one of the stalls to examine it.

"Nothing is here…"

"So, it wasn't sudden then, they had time to grab everything," I replied, making my way over to her. She looked over at me, then spun around to take in her surroundings once more.

"But what the hell is this? Where is everyone?" Just then a loud hiss erupted beneath us, making me and Bastien jump back, backpedaling toward where Mars was standing. I was shocked at what I saw, there was a faint light in the ground where we were standing, and the sand started to glow ever brighter with magnificent displays of orange and yellow as the anomaly seemed to creep closer to us.

I put my arms out in front of my companions, forcing them to take a couple of steps back along with me. I could feel the heat start to radiate from below and the sand started to hiss louder as it seemed to melt around the circle of orange. As I retreated back once more, a man of fire slowly started emerging, from the head to the shoulders and eventually the torso. The flames engulfing the body roared as the unbearable heat nearly made me stumble back as it was pulsing relentlessly from him. I covered my face with my arm in an attempt to shield myself, but the burning sensation only changed locations to my forearm, offering me little reprieve.

With a loud crackle and hiss, the heat suddenly disappeared, and a rush of cooling air returned to me once more. I quickly threw my arm down and saw Lex walking toward us from a shimmering circle in the sand behind him. It made some light crackling sounds as it cooled into a solid ring of glass. I took a step back to ready myself, but instead he simply stopped in his tracks. His familiar yellow eyes stared at us from behind that mask of his.

"I do hope my message has found you well." A low, suave voice finally coming from behind his disguise.

"Yeah. The butterfly was a nice touch," Bastien replied sarcastically. The two had a tense stare down for a rather uncomfortable minute.

"I must apologize for any obscenities you may have witnessed in the canyon. Those under my employ are... passionate," he finally replied, brushing some leftover sand off his shoulder. He must have been talking about the man we saw hung from the tree.

"Quit lying to us with your fake sympathy, Lex." Mars stepped forward, raising her voice at him. I could feel the anger in her words. Lex finished brushing sand off of him and dropped his arms to his sides. He paused for a moment, then slowly turned to face her. His eyes bore into us with an incredible malice. I wasn't sure why, but I felt... afraid. Her words must have offended him.

"I may be a lot of things. But I am not a liar." The force in his words seemed to make Mars's voice escape her body as I heard a faint shudder from her. I felt the same ill intent as her; and right then I realized, we were not going to leave this encounter the same.

Chapter 35

We all stared intently at our foe. I tried to control my breathing so as to not appear too worried. I could feel sweat dripping down my body on the inside of my tunic, and my eyes were burning, but I didn't dare blink. I didn't want to risk that split second of time I wouldn't be able to keep my eyes on him. No one was talking; the situation felt like a standoff, both parties just waiting to see who makes the first move. He didn't seem to be bothered too much by our presence; his demeanor seemed very calm. Either he didn't view us as a threat, or he was an excellent actor.

"I am pleased you all decided to arrive. I am sure you must have realized this chase we are on would never end," Lex spoke up in a calm tone once more, seemingly over the insult that Mars threw at him. I relaxed my hands and took one more look around at the emptiness of the town around us.

"Where is everyone?" I demanded. His yellow eyes behind his mask flicked toward me and stared for a couple of seconds.

"I evacuated them. There is no need for innocents to become involved in our quarrel." I stared at him, unable to formulate a response. It caught me off guard, it sounded almost... noble.

"If our... encounter turns out poorly for you, it wouldn't be wise for them to see the fear in your eyes as you extinguish," he added on.

"We didn't come here out of fear from you, we came here to stop you, to protect others like us!" Bastien stepped forward, yelling at him.

"Your hero complex demands that you present yourself in a valiant light, that you give yourself an imaginary purpose. If you must fabricate a task to give yourself worth, then you have none," he growled, taking a step toward us of his own. I braced myself, preparing for the worst. I didn't see any glow from his hands or see any indication he was going to use his power. Just that same, cold stare. It was becoming ever more apparent that nothing we could say would sway him, he was too far set in his ways.

"Why are we talking, Lex?" I spoke up, turning his attention away from my angry companion. He could've just attacked us outright, gotten the jump on us. So why was he even conversing with us?

"Yes. Why are we?"

I let out a shallow gasp, realizing I might have made a mistake. His tone of voice sounded irritated. I grew tense, and I realized that subconsciously I was stalling for time by talking to him.

"Shall we begin, saviors?" He raised his right arm into the air and gave out a sharp snap of his fingers. I heard footsteps coming from all the buildings behind him, revealing dozens of mercenaries and slavers who were emerging from around the corners, all armed. Eventually, they all lined up behind Lex. There had to have been at least fifty of them, maybe more. The sun glistened off all of the polished blades in their hands.

I took a step back and looked over at Bastien, who was also visibly shocked.

"I realize this isn't ideal for you, but you must understand this is my livelihood. I cannot afford to take chances," Lex spoke in a calm tone and held out his arms as if to show off his small army. I scanned across, trying to wrap my head around how we were going to defend ourselves.

"We can't fight that many," I turned to the other two next to me and said in a hushed tone of voice. They both were staring ahead, ignoring my concerns.

"What are we supposed to do?" I added on, hoping for something, anything, that resembles a plan. The slavers we might have a chance against, but with Lex involved? I didn't like our odds.

Mars slowly stepped toward the amassed force ahead of us, and I saw she had a straight expression on her face. How could she be calm right now? Lex turned his attention toward her, dropping his arms back to his sides.

"Did you really expect him to fight fair?" Mars turned back toward us, her eyes already starting to shimmer a bright green. I opened my mouth, but no words came out. I stood there in anticipation as to what she could possibly do. Once she turned back to our adversaries, she opened her palms outward and took a deep breath.

At least one of us is prepared, she mumbled to herself. I was about to step toward her, but a loud boom followed by a green shockwave crashed outward from her, causing me to stumble back. I threw my arms in front of my face to protect myself and dared a peek as I saw roots starting to grow and ensnare themselves around her feet, making their way up her legs. She was becoming rooted to the ground. Tendrils of vines with blooming flowers started to entangle around her arms and neck before reaching her face. She had her eyes closed.

I darted my gaze back and forth between her and Lex, trying to see what he was going to do. Another boom crashed out of her, and one of the slavers started to step toward her but was stopped by Lex putting his arm out to stop him. He seemed to be just as invested in this power as I was. Finally, she opened her eyes.

211

They were glowing a striking bright green that seemed to be spilling out of her iris and into the whites of her eyes. The booming and shockwaves stopped, and there was an eerie silence. After a tense stare-down between her and the masked Sage across from us, she raised her right hand into the sky. I looked up at her extended arm and gasped at the sight of the sky. It was a pale shade of green, even the sun seemed to be tinted in the same hue.

"How…?" I started, the words tumbling out of my mouth. I was about to ask again, but loud screams echoed from behind us in the distance. Me and Bastien spun around. They were constant and seemed to be emanating from the golden forest up on the cliffs. I could see something spilling over the cliff-side and squinted against the sun to try and make out what it was. I was alarmed when I saw what was happening; at least a hundred dryads, humanoid tree creatures, were sprinting toward us at a frighteningly fast speed. The ground was rumbling as they got closer, and I took a step back in shock. Leaves and dust were exploding outward behind them as they relentlessly sprinted toward us. As they grew closer, I took another step back, but Bastien grabbed my arm to stop me, and I looked back to see Mars thrust her raised arm forward at the slavers. The force of the wave of dryads rushed by us as they sprinted past, toward the clearly alarmed slavers.

Chapter 36

The loud crashing against swords and spears was nearly deafening as the dryads sprinted into the wall of slavers and mercenaries. The sight of blood, branches, and leaves all erupting from the chaos was hard to watch. The shrieking trees were being cut down, but just as many slavers seemed to be getting crushed and thrown around as well.

"Don't just stand there! Go!" I looked over at Mars as she yelled her command at us. She was clearly showing signs of fatigue as her arms started to droop down, and I saw a bead of sweat run down her face. She had to be continuously channeling to control all of them, and it was draining her. I took a step back and turned to make eye contact with Bastien, who gave me a nod and ran toward the large crowd. She quickly materialized two whips of light in her hands, ducking underneath a swinging sword and striking back, creating a bright flash and yelling from the man she struck. Countless flashes quickly followed as she became lost in the fray. I tried my best to keep an eye on her.

I wanted to try and get a better viewpoint, so I moved closer and found myself near the edge of the battle. Bodies of slavers and dryads surrounded me. I wanted to take another step forward, but a slaver had broken away and started charging me, yelling. I didn't see him in time, and only realized he was charging when he had his arm cocked back. I dropped to one knee and threw my arms up in front of me in a vain attempt to protect myself. I didn't have time to think, just react. When I closed my eyes, I heard a loud clang and scraping sound as I felt the blade hit my arms, but I felt nothing. I opened my eyes to see the slaver stumbling, trying to regain his balance. I stood up, confused as I watched him stand back up and face me.

"What the hell have you done?" he yelled at me, angrily. I took a step back and looked down at my left arm. It was covered in bones in what looked to be the shape of a shield. But where did…?

I gasped as I looked around me and realized the bodies of dead slavers around me had been desecrated. Their corpses ripped open. Their bones made my shield… I hadn't realized I had done that; did I do that subconsciously?

Once more I heard him charge me, instead lunging forward ready to impale me with his sword. Again, I reacted by swinging my right arm down to deflect it away, and once again I saw the bones of the dead quickly take shape around my forearm and extend into a blade of my own. With another clang of his metal against bone, he stumbled once more, and I swung up in response, striking him. His body fell limp to the ground behind me, his momentum still carrying him a couple of feet. Blood ran down the edge of my blade as I still held it up high. By now, I had realized what I had done. I slashed him across his torso, deep enough to kill him almost instantly. How were my reflexes doing this? It seemed like my body was making decisions faster than my own mind was.

A couple more flashes and yelling snapped me back to reality, and without a second thought I ran and crashed into the chaos. I fought and fought, swinging my blade and doing my best to deflect incoming attacks against me. I swung at an enemy, but I was too slow; he jumped out of the way, and the weight of my heavy sword made me lose my balance and stumble. I managed to get a look back over my shoulder to see him already swinging his mace toward me. A cold surge of anger ran through me as I watched him fall to the ground, and I saw a corpse at his feet had grabbed his ankle and pulled it, making him trip. Another unintended blip of my powers. But I could feel it all mending with me; like the undead were becoming one with my subconscious. They just… acted in my best interest.

I saw my opportunity and struck the slaver who was struggling to cut the hand of the deceased away from him. I had to act before I could stop and realize what I was doing. I knew it was sickening, but I also knew it was either me, or them. I forced myself back up on my feet, the hot sand sticking to every surface of my skin from the sweat. The scorching sun and the dust being kicked up were suffocating. My head started pounding as my breathing became more labored.

It seemed like an eternity, but between me, Bastien, and Mars's dryads, we finally gained the advantage. It appeared that only about half of the dryads had been cut down, and I turned to watch as Bastien swung her whip one more time to take down the last standing slaver. She keeled over and her whips of light dissipated, breathing heavily before she shakily pushed herself back upright. I walked past the now motionless combative trees, nodding at her as I wiped the sweat from my face. I was exhausted, and she clearly was too.

"Hurry!" Mars yelled from the distance. She was down on one knee now, clenching her teeth and only able to hold one arm up. The green glow around her arm seemed to be dimming; she was nearly at her limit. I turned to face Lex, who had been standing in the back with his arms crossed, watching the battle as it had unfolded. He was alone now, and even though we were exhausted, I suddenly liked our odds. I started walking quickly toward him as the dryads started to move once more, running toward him. This was it; we can finally end this. We can finally go home. We can—

Lex uncrossed his arms and blinding fire started swirling around them, making me stop in my tracks. The dryads sprinted past me, undeterred. I watched in horror as the flames collected into his hands, and he thrust his arms to the ground.

"Wait!" I tried to yell, hoping to stop the dryads from attacking, but I was too late. An eruption of fire blasted out from around him, sending a flaming shockwave through the crowd, engulfing all of them instantly. I threw my shield up at the last second before a blistering heat engulfed me and sent me flying back through the air. The heat was suffocating, and I slammed hard into the wall of a building, the side of my head and shoulder striking the structure, sending me bouncing off and crashing into the ground.

I gasped for air as my head rang and throbbed. I couldn't see straight. My vision was blurry and wobbling. I couldn't move, and my vision tunneled. The most I could do was roll over, and to my dismay I could make out the image of all the dryads shrieking and burning away as they all collapsed to the ground in smoldering heaps. I tried to turn my head and could barely make out the image of Bastien, who was several dozen feet away, struggling to get onto her feet. I forced myself to sit up with a pained grunt, even though my senses were screaming at me not to. My clothes were still smoldering and burning my skin. I heard heavy footsteps approaching me, and I blinked a couple of times while looking up to focus my vision.

Lex was standing over me. Before I could react, his hand was grasped around my neck, lifting me up off the ground.

Chapter 37

I struggled as my fists were slamming into his arm, desperately trying to get some sort of gasp or reprieve from his grip. His skin felt scorching to the touch, and the stinging pain was quickly becoming unbearable.

"Disappointing. I thought you would put up more of a fight than this," he growled at me. I opened my eyes through my gritted teeth and saw him glaring at me from behind his mask. I kept trying to somehow focus long enough to conjure up something, but every time I got close, it would slip away. I couldn't focus, couldn't think about anything but trying to breathe. I could feel myself growing weaker as it became harder to maintain a tight enough grip on his arm. As my hands were about to drop, I saw a bright flash from the corner of my eye, and I was dropped to the ground. I rolled onto my hands and knees and started coughing, desperately trying to suck in as much air as possible.

"Get your god damn hands off him!" I heard Bastien yell. I managed to turn my head to see the blurry outline of her and Mars standing next to each other. I shakily tried to get up on one knee, but nearly fell back over in the process. I had to keep fighting, even though every limb in my body was screaming in protest.

"Finally," Lex replied to her, turning to face their direction. He had his back to me. He clearly did not think I was any sort of threat. The thought of that disrespect made me angry, I had to show him how blinded by his arrogance he really was.

A grunt and a loud shimmering sound made me look toward my companions. My vision was finally starting to clear, and I saw Bastien throw what looked like a large, spinning shuriken of light at him, which he ducked to avoid. I could feel the energy of it as it flew past me with a loud 'buzzing' sound. Mars let out a loud yell as several large roots burst from the sand beneath us, swinging at Lex. As one was about to strike him, he engulfed his body in flames as he was hit, sending him sliding back a couple of feet. The root burned away where it had made contact, creating enough damage for it to snap in half, falling limp to the sand with a loud thud.

I was still struggling to catch my breath, but I had finally managed to stand on my own two feet. Before I could even think about doing anything else though, I heard the familiar buzzing sound of the shuriken return, and I looked up at the sky. It must have risen above the buildings and swooped back around and was now in a full-on dive toward him once more. I watched in anticipation, hoping that he might not see it in time, but my hopes were quickly dashed as he spun around, striking it with a fireball and sending it flying off course and slicing into a building.

Mars was already sprinting toward him, and I watched as her body started to change. Her skin turned green and was breaking apart, turning into thousands of small leaves. I couldn't do anything but watch her body split into several leafy clones of herself, all sprinting toward him. Lex scoffed as he brandished an axe made of flames and swung at Mars, slicing her body in half. I nearly yelled in horror, but I caught myself as I watched her body burst apart and the individual leaves blow away in the wind. Me and Lex both looked on confused, and I heard a yell coming from behind him as Mars materialized out of one of her clones and plunged a dagger she had hidden in her trousers. He yelled in pain as he swung his flaming axe around, barely missing her.

I saw my opportunity, I had to act. I forced my legs to run forward, the anger swelling inside me. I could feel the familiar feeling of cold rushing through my arms and into my body, and I held out my hand toward him, bursting forth that violet smoke I had manifested in the past. Almost as if on instinct, I clenched my fists and the smoke formed into the rough shape of an enormous scythe. I let out a yell of my own as I forced it to swing toward him with reckless abandon, smoke billowing out from behind the blade as it ripped through the air. He spun around once more and grabbed it with flaming hands, causing him to slide backward through the sand as we struggled to overpower each other. Mars must have seen this as an opportunity, because she burst forth more roots from beneath the ground, ensnaring his lower body, immobilizing him. I still struggled to push my scythe through and felt him losing ground from our attacks. I felt I could overpower him, channel more of my power into my attack. No, I knew I could. But something was stopping me, holding me back, like I had hit a wall. I kept trying, desperate to break past my limit, but I kept getting held back. I let out a yell as my frustration grew. I had to stop him.

Seemingly out of nowhere, Bastien leapt over my blade, her hand covered in a blinding light. Lex barely had time to try and contort his body out of the way, and Bastien's fist still managed to make a striking blow. She fell to the ground past him and immediately jumped on her feet, with a shocked expression on her face. In fact, we were all shocked. Half of Lex's mask had been broken clean through as it crumbled to the sandy ground below. I saw the left side of his face, his skin had burn scars in several spots. But I could see his expressions now as well, he looked surprised, then angry, then outright rage. He let out a deafening roar as his body erupted into fire, my scythe being dematerialized, and Mars's roots burned. Even the dagger embedded in his back melted away. I stumbled back as the air itself seemed to ignite around him. Quickly, though, he extinguished himself, the edges of his clothing still smoldering.

"Fine. You've shown me what you can do, now I'll show you what I can do," he said, laughing. I took another step back at his words, was he really not giving it his all? As those thoughts ran though my head, he held his hands out to his side, and I watched as a dozen pikes of fire formed out of thin air in the sky above the buildings. They looked to each be at least five feet long. I gasped as I watched in horror, the large pikes growing brighter above me. I was frantically trying to figure out what he was going to do.

With one more laugh, he thrust his arms down, sending the flaming rods crashing into the ground, narrowly missing me and the others. The ground shook at each impact, and I watched as the top of them all started glowing brighter and brighter.

"Get down!" I yelled, and thankfully all three of us dove to the ground just in time as the thin orange lines exploded from the top of each pike, cleaving through and slicing the entire town in half. I watched in horror from the sand as several buildings collapsed from the decimation. Everything was shaking, and the dust and smoke were blinding. I coughed and jumped to my feet as I tried to look through the carnage for any sign of my companions. As the smoke started to clear, I could see the upper body of Bastien collapsed on the ground, her legs buried underneath the remains of a collapsed building. I tried to run over to her, but another red glow erupted from the smoke, striking me on the side and sending me flying through the street. I tumbled and slid all the way to the edge of the town, pain radiating through every limb. My head was pounding. I grabbed my arm that had been struck, my skin was burning, and the awful smell of seared flesh stung my nostrils. I wanted to lay there and wither away. My whole life I wanted to curl up and recede away from anything resembling conflict and pain. I hated it about myself and was scolded for it by my family. I remembered my mom calling me, "Weak, sensitive." Her words always filled me with rage. I wanted to prove her wrong, but I never did. If she saw me right now, would she say the same thing?

A loud scream pierced the air, jolting my eyes open. My vision was blurry again, but after a moment, it cleared up enough to see what was going on. I turned my head back into the demolished town and saw Mars. Lex was holding her against the ruined wall of one of the buildings, his hand burning her arm as he held her back. She was screaming in pain; he was going to kill her. I forced myself once more to my knees, struggling to think of what to do. I was too injured to even run, and after seeing what he just did, I knew I wouldn't stand a chance against him. But even still, I had to try... I had to do something.

I pushed myself up onto one knee and heard an object fall to the ground next to me. I looked down to see the rusted, engraved dagger that I had been carrying around with me. I reached out and grasped it into my palm, staring at the blade once more. It whispered to me again, just like before. But... I could understand it now.

"Unleash... power..." I stared in amazement. It wasn't speaking verbally, it was... in my head.

"Take... life..." Its sentences were broken, incomplete. I tried to understand. Why was it saying this...? Why—

I suddenly remembered from the nightmare where I obtained

221

this weapon, one last phrase the decrepit hand spoke to me, "Death cannot fully follow the living." I didn't understand it at first, but… was this why I felt myself become hindered? Unable to surpass my limits? Because I was… alive?

"… Yes…" The dagger hissed as it seemed to respond to my thoughts, and I dropped it in shock. No, I couldn't, that's asking too much. Just then, even Mars's own words from days before echoed in my head, *Maybe you're just too alive.* She meant it as a joke, but maybe she was right. I stared down at it, fear consuming me at the realization of unlocking my true potential.

Mars's screams snapped me out of my trance, and I saw her once more being tortured. Tears swelled up in my eyes, and with a trembling hand I reached down and grabbed the dagger once more. I knew what I had to do, but I didn't know if I was strong enough to do it. I choked on my own tears as I held the blade up to my throat, I wanted to sob from the amount of fear I was in. How could this be the decision I was given? How was this fair? The blade vibrated almost eagerly in my hand. Her screams pierced my ears once more, and I stared at her as she writhed in pain. I started sobbing as my hand started shaking, the blade trembling against my neck. I had to do it, if not for me, then for her. Anything to save her. I screamed through my tears as I sliced the blade across my throat.

Anything.

Chapter 38

The intense burning on my neck quickly turned to pain, and I could feel a hot liquid dribbling down my body. I sat there on my knees staring up at the clouds, numb from my decision. I wanted to cry, but I couldn't. The pain wouldn't afford me that luxury. I felt my body become weaker, followed by nausea. My vision was starting to tunnel. I waited for the inevitable, fear flooding over me. I knew it had to be any second now. It almost felt freeing. I closed my eyes.

A sharp sound pierced my ears as I quickly opened my eyes once more. It sounded like something being engraved in stone. Upon looking down, I saw it. The blood from my throat, my own blood. It wasn't running down my body, it was floating outward away from me on its own before falling into a runic pattern all around me. It sizzled into the sand before hardening into a shiny black design. I painfully turned to look around me; what was this? Was this the same symbol etched into the dagger...? The dagger... I looked down at my hand, seeing my tunic only having a couple of drops of a dark red stain, while my trousers being visibly dirty but free of any blood. And the rusted blade I just used was... gone. My eyes suddenly shot open at the realization that my pain was subsiding, and why was I even conscious...?

The black symbol continued to harden around me until I watched one last drop of my blood fall into the design around me, and I screamed. My vision turned red, my heart and head were pounding faster and faster, and my body felt as if I was being crushed from every direction. I keeled over and fell to my side; the intensity was unrelenting. I couldn't breathe, and every breath I managed to get was ripped away by me yelling. I writhed on the ground, feeling waves of cold and heat pulsate through me. I opened my eyes to see my dark red vision once more. But my skin… It looked as if it was… changing. My nails were growing darker, and that familiar purple mist started swirling around my extremities. I rolled over onto my knees, desperate to find some position that offered me some sort of relief, but it never came. As I lay there gasping for air in between the ruthless pain, some kind of force snapped me into the upright position, making a sickening sound in my spine which radiated a whole new pain throughout my body as the mist started engulfing the rest of me. I let out another scream, but it was different. It was extremely high-pitched, deafening, ear-splitting. My eyes widened as I was forced to face the sky, black tendrils invading the edges of my vision before blinding me completely. The ground seemed to open up beneath me, and I fell.

I awoke on my back with a raspy gasp as I coughed and wheezed. I rolled over, wanting to vomit but nothing came; I dry heaved painfully as I audibly inhaled to catch my breath afterward. I lay there for a moment, trying to collect myself from the intense trauma I had just endured. What was that? Why didn't I die…? I immediately grasped my throat, and to my shock, felt a rather large scar that had healed over. Was that it? Did I—

I sat up, eager to see the ruined town once more. But upon opening my eyes, I found myself elsewhere. I was in a long hallway, with several doors and dusty lamps hung from the walls. The wood floor beneath me was stained and looked like it hadn't been upkept in ages, with walls made of similar wood planks. I sat there, looking around for several minutes. I didn't know where I was and yet… why did this place seem familiar?

The wood creaked as I stood up, and my footsteps seemed to be muffled. I spun around, seeing an endless black expanse behind me and a single brown door at the other end of the hallway.

"Hello?" I called out. My voice sounded suppressed, and the words were barely audible. All of my movements seemed slowed, like I was currently underwater. Every muscle I moved was a struggle. I opened my mouth to speak once more but was interrupted by the sound of a lock clicking behind me. I slowly spun around to face the door at the far end of the hallway and waited. After a couple of seconds, it slowly creaked open, and a child with a blurry face emerged before the door creaked shut and closed behind them. I stared in confusion, and it felt like they were staring back. I tried to move toward them, but I couldn't. It felt as if there was a barrier in my way, blocking me. I pressed my hands against it and pushed to no avail. It was as if I was behind a glass wall. I had hardly noticed the child had started walking toward me while I was preoccupied with the barrier in my way. But there I stood, watching them come closer, their face becoming more and more clear the nearer they came. I stood in silence until they stopped a couple of feet in front of me, and I gasped. It was… me.

But… me as a child. No more than five. He was wearing a dirty tunic with linen shirt underneath and equally dirty brown trousers. One of the knees was ripped open, showing scraped up skin as if he had just been playing. His unkempt hair was strikingly how I had mine at his age. I stood there dumbfounded, observing every detail about him. But the biggest shock was when I scanned his face once more. He was bruised, his left cheek had a purple mark and so did his left eye. And he was crying.

Tears were streaming down his face as he stood, staring at me, motionless.

"What happened?" I tried to speak, but my voice was once more drowned out and muffled. He slowly shook his head at me before wiping away his tears before slowly looking back up to meet my gaze. I wanted to speak to him, wanted to find out what was going on. I tried to speak again, but as I did, a bright white and silver glow started beneath his feet, and I watched as silver flames slowly started to grow from below him. I stood there, silent as the flames rose higher and higher, engulfing his feet, then his legs. He stood there, not breaking his gaze away from me. I watched in agony as an overwhelming sense of dread and sadness washed over me. I shouted and pounded against the barrier in front of me, frustratingly soft from my movement being slowed. I started to cry myself as I watched the flames completely consume his entire being. I yelled once more as I stood there, helpless. The beautiful silver flames haunted me as they burned. Soon, his torso was covered, then his face. I made eye contact with myself one last time as tears streamed down both of our cheeks. He was engulfed, a flickering silver ember in front of me. I didn't understand what was happening.

I felt defeated and dropped to my knees, cursing my helplessness. I let out one more muffled yell and the worn wooden floor gave way beneath me. Wooden boards snapped in two and tumbled into the darkness below, and I too fell into the abyss.

I watched motionless as the hallway drifted farther and farther away as I sank deeper. The sorrow still overwhelming me, and I blinked slowly. I felt helpless, again. I couldn't save him. Save... me. I hated this feeling. I hated being like this. Always unable to help those I cherish. The sorrow quickly turned to anger as I clenched my fists. No, no more. I was done being like this. Done being helpless. My anger turned into a blind rage as I clenched my teeth. Emotions and a chilling cold swirled inside me before spilling out around me. The black abyss started to rumble, then swirl around me in a vortex. Black tendrils quickly started snaking up my arms, covering my torso, neck and then my face. My rage spilled out as I let out the loudest yell I could muster. The black tendrils covered my vision once more, the abyss engulfing me.

When it broke away, I was once more on my knees, the burning sand hissing against my skin. I was trembling, my breath deep and heavy. I opened my eyes, my vision flooded with a dark red hue. And my skin… was a different shade as well. It looked almost… gray. Blood was dribbling out of the corners of my mouth and eyes, dropping onto the ground beneath me. But most striking of all was the power I felt. Like I was floating in an endless ocean. And it was all mine. I felt it pouring out of me, it was intoxicating, like I could crack the world itself. I rose up to my feet in a fluid motion before floating a couple of inches off the ground and let out another blood-curdling high-pitched screech.

My vision shot up, and I made eye contact with Lex, who had dropped an unconscious Mars to the ground. He was staring at me, shocked. I could see a bright light coming from his chest, and I knew it was his soul. It was beckoning to me, like a moth to a flame. Mars had a bright glow emanating from her as well, but I only cared about him. Hatred and hunger ravaged through me, and only one word ran through my mind. Kill. With one more screech, I dashed toward him.

Chapter 39

I flew toward him with no thoughts or any regard for anything else. My mind was on a linear path to his destruction. Lex immediately sent forth a continuous stream of fire at me, and I struck it head-on. I could smell my skin melting, but I felt no pain. I felt no hesitation. And he soon realized that as well because he crossed his arms in front of him to brace, and I smashed into his body, driving my shoulder into his torso. The force of my momentum drove us both through the wall of a half-destroyed building behind him. Brick and dust exploded into the air as I threw him further back, causing him to tumble on the wooden floor and over the leftover debris of someone's home. I stood there, rage pulsing through me, causing me to pace back and forth. I glared him down when he finally looked up, a horrified expression showing through the exposed half of his mask. The gray skin on my body made sickening squelching sounds as it reconnected and restored itself back to normal from the severe burns I had suffered only moments before.

Get up, I growled in my mind. He had to answer for everything he had done. He had to make this worthwhile.

GET. UP, my voice now yelling in my mind. I didn't vocalize my demands, only letting out another glass-shattering screech. Lex jumped back on his feet, his attire covered in dirt and torn apart, a steady stream of blood trickling down his arm from a cut he had just suffered. I lunged forward once more, not giving him a moment's reprieve. He grabbed my hands in his own and we locked arms, each trying to push the other back. His breathing was labored, and his arms trembled as he lost ground to me. I knew he couldn't fight me off, and I pushed him slowly back, more and more.

Lex let out a yell and a dome of fire erupted around him. I released my grip and jumped back, frustration building inside me. I could still see his soul glowing through the thick flames between us, and I slowly walked toward him, the flames scorching me but once again having no effect. I nearly reached him once more before he let out another yell and erupted into a blazing tornado of fire that ripped through the roof that was still standing, sending him soaring into the upper reaches of the vortex. I stood on the ground, watching him climb higher and higher.

"No. NO. YOU ARE MINE," I yelled out, several dozen mouths of the damned creating my voice. He would not get away from me. I reached out to the mass amounts of bodies strewn throughout the town, their bodies bursting open as bone, skin, and sinew flew toward me, forming into massive, webbed wings of bone on my back. I crouched and jumped into the sky, my wings of the dead booming with every flap behind me. I quickly climbed higher to him, following the glow of his soul until I crashed through his vortex, looking into his eyes. Fear quickly flooded his face as I grabbed him, tackling him out of the fire, sending us tumbling through the air and back down to the ruins below.

We exchanged several punches as we spun through the air in our freefall. His flaming powers bouncing off me with no effect.

"What... are you?" he yelled, trying to fight me off him. I didn't answer, but instead gained control and rolled him underneath me as I jumped off his chest, sending him crashing into the shattered, wooden remains of The Winking Quail. My wings made a couple more booms as I slowed my descent to land gently on the mangled floor of the pub. The stump of Mars's tree she had burst through the floor before was still present to my left, with evidence of repairs starting to surround the since chopped down giant. As the dust settled, I saw my prey. He was lying on his back, coughing. A shattered wooden table leg was protruding through his chest, blood covering the splintered end. I floated toward him, growling as I savored this moment. Blood was running from the edge of his mouth as he struggled to open his eyes, once more seeing me looming over him. I quickly snatched his face in my hand, forcing his head to turn and face me directly as he grunted in pain.

"How can God… allow you to exist?" He choked out the words, his voice was weak. I leaned closer toward him, his yellow eyes mere inches away. God? No deity could hope to stand against me now.

"Because he fears me."

"… Finish this then… let me… be with my son once more." I wanted to kill him; his life was in the palm of my hand. I placed my open hand on his chest to rip his soul out, but… I hesitated. I blinked a couple of times, the deep red hue of my vision rippling. What did he say…?

"Please…" He choked on more blood. I stared deep into his eyes, and I saw true sorrow, regret. He was so afraid. Afraid of me. A tear escaped his eye and rolled down his cheek. What have I done? Was I so blinded by my rage that I took his mantle of becoming the monster…? I opened my mouth to speak, but an unrelenting pain throbbed in my head, radiating throughout my body. I wanted to scream, but I stumbled and was soon once more filled with my primal rage. I didn't hesitate a second longer, I ripped out his soul. The silky white essence swirled around my hand as I watched his life get snuffed from his eyes. I absorbed every ounce of his soul, an incredible strength surging throughout. I let out another high-pitched screech as his now lifeless husk laid motionless beneath me.

"Sid...?" I whirled around, seeing Bastien in the still standing doorway of the pub, one hand holding herself upright against the frame, the other clutching her ribs. A shocked expression was on her face as she seemingly struggled to come to terms with what she was witnessing.

"What have you...?" Her voice trembling. I slowly floated toward her; the familiar rage once more surging through me as I looked down upon her.

Chapter 40

I floated toward her, the rage inside still ravaging throughout. I didn't know why I felt so much desire to destroy, but I didn't care. No one would stand in my way. No one would stop me.

"Sid... stop," she said, backing away from me slowly. A faint shimmer of light started to manifest in her right hand, glowing brighter. I didn't stop. I could only focus on the glow of her soul, it was so close, and I wanted it.

"You killed Lex. We won. It's over..." she added on, pleading with me as she continued to back away, I stopped, hearing the words that had come from her. She was right, I did win. But it will never be over, not for me. I craved more. Before another thought could run through my head, I lunged forward, ready to strike against her. At the last second, a shield of light burst forth from her hand, deflecting me and bouncing me back. She had fallen to the ground, as had I. But I was quickly back on my feet, ready to attack again. She looked at me from the ground with a scared expression on her face and began gathering light in her hands once more.

I was about to lunge forward again, but... out of the corner of my eye, I saw movement. I snapped my gaze over, only to see Mars sitting up, holding her left arm. She was staring at me. She looked horrified as I met her gaze.

"Sid... don't," Bastien pleaded, noticing that I realized Mars was present as well. But I didn't feel rage, or hunger, I felt... something else. A heartbeat. I hadn't felt it since I transformed.

My vision became less saturated, it lightened, cleared. She... I had to... approach her. I slowly floated toward her, blinking a couple of times, the heartbeat in my chest causing a pulsing pain in my chest. What was happening to me...? I groaned through the monstrous growl that I let out. She started to backpedal away once she noticed I was coming for her.

"Sid!" I heard Bastien yell behind me. A bright shower of light behind me cast a long shadow in every direction. I ignored her and continued on my slow floating march. Mars eventually backed up against the foundation of a building, still refusing to take her eyes off me. Mars needed help, she...

"STOP!" Bastien yelled at the top of her lungs.

I reached out toward Mars, unsure of what I was even going to do. But before I could touch her, a long spear of light ripped through me, penetrating my back and exiting through my chest. I looked down at copious amounts of black liquid pouring from my wound. The spear dissipated almost immediately. I didn't feel pain but... I couldn't move, I felt so weak. My power and strength felt as if they were leaking out. I fell to my feet, then to my knees. I struggled to maintain my balance as the dirt and sand beneath became more and more stained with the black ichor. My skin was rippling, it was... changing from gray to its original complexion. I struggled to lift my head and made eye contact with Mars. She was so close. My vision was growing blurry.

"I'm—" I started to speak, but choked on the blood that spilled out of my mouth. I felt as if I was drowning; pain started to show itself once more as I returned back to my normal form.

"What...?" She leaned forward onto her knees, reaching out a hand to my cheek. I blinked a couple more times, desperate to clear up my vision. I wheezed heavily as I struggled to breathe. I could see... the dead beneath me. Dozens of them, all holding out their hands toward me. And beneath them, a familiar black abyss. I forced my head up once more to look her in the eyes. Tears swelling up and running down my cheeks.

"I'm sorry." I used every ounce of strength I had to muster those words to her. I knew I was dying, but I had to tell her. She was the only thing I cared about now. Her eyes grew big, and my limbs gave out. I collapsed into the open hands of the souls beneath me. Into the abyss, I fell.

Printed in the USA
CPSIA information can be obtained
at www.ICGtesting.com
LVHW090719270924
792085LV00002B/15